Lost Girls
Short Stories

ELLEN BIRKETT MORRIS

Relax. Read. Repeat.

LOST GIRLS
By Ellen Birkett Morris
Published by TouchPoint Press
Brookland, AR 72417
www.touchpointpress.com

Copyright © 2020 Ellen Birkett Morris
All rights reserved.

ISBN-13: 978-1-952816-01-7

Editor: Kimberly Coghlan
Cover Design: Colbie Myles

Visit the author's website https://ellenbirkettmorris.ink

First Edition

Printed in the United States of America.

For Bud with all my love, Liz and John for the strong start, my wonderful sisters, Lynn and Julie, and my brave women friends who made it to the other side of girlhood with courage, grit and grace.

Lost Girls appeared in *The Pedestal Magazine*.
Religion appeared in *Antioch Review* and was nominated for a Pushcart Prize.
Harvest appeared in *Sliver of Stone*.
Life After appeared in *The Tishman Review*.
After the Fall appeared in *Alimentum*.
A Rumor of Fire appeared in *Pioneer Town*.
Bottle Tree Blues appeared in *Sawmill Magazine*.
Helter Skelter appeared in *Paradigm*.
Heavy Metal appeared in *Santa Fe Literary Review*.
Fear of Heights appeared in *Inscape*.
Emoticon appeared in *Lunch Ticket*.
Kodachrome appeared in *Notre Dame Review*.
Swimming appeared in *South Carolina Review*.
Neverland appeared in *Richmond Independent Press*
Like I Miss Not Being a Ballerina appeared in *Sou'wester*

Lost Girls

When I was eighteen, thirteen-year-old Dana Lampton disappeared from the strip mall across from her family's apartment. My mind should have been on other things—guys, college, getting past ID checker at the door of the club—but Dana's disappearance captured my attention. We lived in the same neighborhood, and the nearness of the crime creeped me out.

As a kid, even before Dana disappeared, I was sure that I would be the girl that was taken. I was always on edge, waiting for the next catastrophe—the next fight, my dad moving out, my world collapsing around me as my mother cried day after day.

With me gone, those "Don't tell your father" shopping trips wouldn't have happened. My dad wouldn't have anyone to complain to about my mom either— her "stupidity", her "tackiness."

Not that anyone would notice if I was gone. My parents were so busy fighting that a change of scenery would have been appealing, at times. Why not abduction? The kidnapping of Patty Hearst made the possibility seem even more real to me. Forget the fact that my family had trouble putting together enough money to take a family vacation or buy a new car— much less raise a pile of ransom money. After Patty was taken, any middle-aged man walking down my street with his hands in his pockets was cause for alarm.

I almost freaked when my new friend's hippie dad pulled up to the yard where we were playing and yelled for us to get into the van. Images of child slavery rolled through my head. I'd be kept in some commune, forced to mix batches of granola and make homemade yogurt day and night.

I even dreamed about being kidnapped. My captor bore a striking resemblance to the 70s television character Archie Bunker. In the dream, his mother, a kindly gray-haired lady, offered me cake. I woke up in a cold sweat, convinced I had tasted the icing.

As time passed, I realized that I was just too old to be kidnapped anymore. Dana had taken my place. When she came up missing, the FBI combed every inch of the nearby field. The local paper ran her picture once a week for the first year. When I saw her parents on the television, arm in arm, united in their grief, I had a flash of envy. My parents had divorced four years before, wrapped up in their own lives.

While I tried to figure out high school and how keep my grades up on my own, my parents requested my presence for drunken, midnight weeping sessions and second marriages. I always showed up.

Years went by, and still there was no sign of Dana. How does somebody just vanish? In my imagination, I see her getting older, locked in at night, moving from apartment to apartment. Somebody's prize.

And me, on the outside, following my usual routine. School, dates, graduation, college, first job. Sometimes I feel like I'm living for the both of us. I stop and look around, noticing my freedom, the feeling of the sun on my face, my ability to hop in my car and go wherever I want.

Why Dana? I could only guess it was an accident of timing. Who knows how often we cruise the aisles of the grocery store next to a sex offender or drive away from the convenience store as a robber pulls into the lot?

Is it fate? Karma? There are no free rides; that's for sure. All we can do is watch our backs and hope for the best. I can't seem to forget her. Each birthday, I do a quick calculation comparing her would-be age to my own. Every few years, I come here and leave something for Dana— tampons, an old set of car keys, a graduation cap. She'll be 21 this year.

Tonight I'll leave this bottle of Jack Daniel's. By morning it'll be gone.

Inheritance

Some people are born to sin; others inherit it. I didn't know which of these I was until I crossed paths with the Cabots.

The room smelled of lemons and vinegar. Alma Cabot lay stiff across her cherry Duncan Phyfe table. A tall woman, her legs almost reached the end of the table. Her face was slack where it was usually stern, but still, there was no trace of softness.

The table had a high shine. We didn't own a mirror. When I looked down, my reflection startled me. My hair hung in wild tendrils around my face. My eyes were hard. I'd been sitting with the dead woman for fifteen minutes according to the grandfather clock in the corner.

Mrs. Cabot wore her best dress, purple brocade with pearl buttons and matching earrings. I was sure her son Daniel would relieve her of these before her body went into the ground. I heard pearls came from a grain of sand that irritated the oyster. I wasn't surprised that this was Mrs. Cabot's jewelry of choice.

Though she had absented her body, I half expected Mrs. Cabot to pop up and start talking about the fine wood finish, turned edges, and four-legged base of the table. She loved ownership and often spoke about the "fine pieces" her grandmother had brought over from England. She told these stories to anyone who would listen, including my Mama, who spent years mopping the Cabot's floors and cooking their dinner—and then went home to a bed of straw ticking. If I had been my mother, I would have spit in the Cabot's food—or worse, but my mother played by the rules, ones that were set and broken by the Cabots. Because the Cabots had money, nobody said a thing. Mama believed in God's final judgment, but I wasn't sure it was wise to leave it up to Him, what with his reputation for mercy and all.

Mrs. Cabot would have squirmed at the thought of being laid out on her elegant table, though that was the custom around these parts. I wouldn't be seated at this table if she hadn't passed.

I was here for one reason, to take away her sins. My granny had been a sin eater, as her granny was before her, a custom from England that came with her across the ocean along with the family's meager belongings. Part of me thought the ritual was foolishness, though I never said so. The other part of me feared it was real and wondered about the weight of my granny's soul.

Before she died, Granny wrapped up her black cloak and left instructions with Mamma that it was to be passed on to me. I liked to believe she thought I was tough enough to handle the job and smart enough not to take it too seriously. Either way, I'd been bearing the sins of the Cabots for a while now.

I was born on the wrong side of the river, in the elbow, a patch of land by the bend prone to flooding. It was the kind of place people with no sense, or no money, lived. It took my family several generations before Daddy finally built the house up off the ground. So then, when it rained, we were on a dirtier version of Noah's Ark, one with nearly as many inhabitants (Mama, Daddy, me, the twins, four feral cats, three dogs, a chicken and two songbirds). With less food, of course.

Daniel Cabot had crossed the creek to fetch me that morning. It wasn't his first visit. That was shortly after I turned 16, the summer that it flooded and our crops washed out. We almost starved that summer. Daddy let Daniel in and sent him to my room. I didn't know what was happening, but Daddy stood in my doorway and told me to make Daniel welcome; then he closed the door. Daniel stood still, looking at me. I saw his lust, but also a look like he was judging cattle. For all his looking, I don't think he saw me at all. Then he lifted my gown over my head and carried me to the bed.

He was his mother's son, greedy and prideful. He panted as he took me from behind. I stared at the water stain on the wall. It was big and yellowed with ragged brown edges in the shape of a dog. When I was little, I pretended it was real and called it Yeller, which always made my Mama laugh. While Daniel labored, I imagined running through a wide field with Yeller, someplace far away from the elbow.

Daniel pressed his finger against my teeth until I figured I was meant to suck on it, which I did, though I fantasized about biting it off and feeding it to Yeller. At first, I gagged, but then I pretended it was a piece of ice melting in my mouth until it disappeared into nothing.

The Cabots owned the coalmine, but Daniel's finger was as soft as a baby's, unstained by labor. The nail was clean, though raggedy from his chewing it. He smelled of expensive soap, a sharp citrus smell that would come to signal danger to me. I said nothing while he spent his energy on me. I barely moved, hoping he'd get bored and move on. That night, and every visit after, he left fifty cents on my dresser. I never touched the money, but it always disappeared.

I was proud of myself for not crying out that night—or the many nights after. He would have wanted me to whimper and moan. But I didn't want to wake the little ones and stain their first memories with sounds of suffering. When he left, I rinsed my mouth at the washbasin and ran wet rags across my thighs. The rags came back bloody. The next morning Ma washed the stains from my sheets without a word.

This morning, Daniel had stood in the doorway and said, "Mama's dead. The corpse cakes are in the oven, and we need you down at the house."

I dressed quickly in my cloak and took a fine linen handkerchief from Ma's drawer. When we got to the house, I placed the handkerchief on the doorstep. I would retrieve it and the money when my work was done.

Daniel had pushed me roughly in the direction of the dining room and left me alone with her, while he went to fetch his brother. I knew Abraham by reputation only. He had been away at school and then opened a law practice in Charleston.

I walked around the room, running my finger across the scrolls and leaves of the carved sideboard. I slid open a drawer to find linens embroidered with sprigs of lavender. A small sachet of lavender was in the corner of the drawer. I held it to my nose; the sharp, fresh scent reminded me that just outside these walls, the fields were bursting with life. I went back to the table and sat across from Mrs. Cabot, where I could see her face as it slowly turned to stone.

I had been a sin eater before, but that family was strangers to me, folks who had come into the mining camps from Pittsburgh and lost their daughter to the flu. I wondered how much sin she could have accumulated in her five years, not much I would reckon, but the family was superstitious and wanted to send her off to the afterlife with a clean slate. The girl had taken up only a small portion of the table. A corpse cake had laid on her small chest. I said the words, and the mother handed me the cake. The cake had raisins and currants inside and crumbled in my mouth. The family watched as I ate every crumb. When I got outside, two dollars sat on my handkerchief.

I waited until I got into the woods to stick my finger down my throat. A volcano of sweet cake and fruit left a mess in the grass. It was no time at all before the bees came buzzing around it. I figured I'd only taken in a little of the sin, nothing mortal, nothing that would keep me from heaven.

I was jumpy today, my stomach a strange mix of nausea

and hunger. I was used to hunger, but the nausea was a more recent development. I had been waking up with my stomach roiling around. I kept a few peppermint leaves inside my pillow and chewed on them when things got bad.

I ran my hand around the smooth edge of the table. I could do anything now—carve my initials into the underside with my pocket knife, slide the silver sugar shell into my pocket, take a piece of the old woman's hair for some kind of hex. But instead, I touched my stomach and whispered in the dead woman's ear, "I'm carrying your grandchild."

Nobody could tell yet. The small swell in my belly was hidden by my dress. But my state would reveal itself soon—and there would be hell to pay. I looked out the window at the tall oak standing in front of the house. It was a huge old tree with a gnarled trunk. The thick branches came out like tentacles spreading toward the sun, taking up space against the sky. I saw a strong, low branch, a perfect place to perch and watch the world, and I took in the sturdy branches just beyond, footholds to the sky. My son would never play there.

I heard the back door close, and I sat back quickly and raised the hood of my cloak to cover my face. Daniel pushed the door open, a plate of cakes in his hand, and he held it for another man. Abraham was tall and resembled Daniel around the nose and forehead, but he had much kinder eyes.

He reached his hand out toward me.

"Don't bother," said Daniel.

The man raised his eyebrows. I held back a smile.

9

Abraham looked at his mother. "She's not here. There is no trace of her," he said, quietly.

"Only death could still the likes of her," said Daniel.

"What is this?" asked Abraham, nodding at me.

"A local burial custom of the rabble, some malarkey about eating the sins of the deceased. Mother insisted we do it if she should die."

If she should die! Did the Cabots think immortality was theirs for a price, like everything else?

Daniel laid the plate of cakes on his mother's still chest.

The cakes were round and small and black around the edges.

The brothers looked at me expectantly.

I picked up a cake and held it to my mouth. When my teeth bit down, I felt like a vulture feasting on the entrails of some small, soft animal that had gotten in the way, but I knew I was that small, soft animal and Daniel wouldn't quit visiting me at night until nothing was left of me but a crimson stain on the floor. I chewed and swallowed, felt the hard cake scrape down my throat.

I heard myself speak, though in my mind, I was far above the house, circling, waiting for my chance to pounce. My voice was loud and strong.

"I pledge my soul for your sins and ask that God Almighty remove those sins from you and place them up on me, and I eat this food to show that I have taken your sins upon me. If I lie, may God strike me dead."

I looked at the brothers, whose eyes were closed. It was done. I walked to the door. I could see the coins shining on my handkerchief. I bent down to scoop them up. I felt a presence behind me. Abraham stepped forward and pressed five dollars into my hands. I looked him in the face, wondering if my son would look like him.

It was enough money for the train east. I could be alone with my sins. I'd find a place somewhere, get a dog, and take in sewing. I would be free. My son would live unencumbered by legacy, free in a way I could only imagine. I walked quickly through the woods, stopping only to put my finger down my throat.

I rushed home and began to pack. I took my two dresses, crochet hook, and knitting needles and the skein of yarn I had been saving to make mittens for the twins. I stopped to touch the stain on the wall, which, in the light of day, looked like nothing but a dirty spot.

Mama stood in my doorway. "Don't," she said.

"I've got to." My hand wandered to the five dollars folded in my pockets. I looked into her face and noticed the lines worn into its surface, the hollows of her checks.

"We'll starve."

If I stayed, I would become her, more indebted to the Cabots with each passing day, for whatever table scraps they decided to throw my way, like a dog—worse than a dog, since I was more than my appetites.

I pushed past her and ran out the door. I ran all the way to town and bought a ticket to Richmond. I barely had time to sit down before the train pulled up. It was my first time on a train. The seats were covered in leather, and the interior was trimmed in wood. I knew I stood out in my simple dress and mended shawl. I took a seat near the door. It wasn't long before the rocking of the cars lulled me to sleep. It was a dreamless sleep, not like my dreams at home, where I was forever trying to escape from some unknown pursuer.

I woke up as a man made his way down the aisle with a trolley that carried a teakettle and cake. "Refreshment, Miss?"

I had a cup of tea with cream and sugar. I sipped it slowly. When I got settled, this would be my new ritual—a cup of tea in the quiet of the afternoon while the baby slept. Prince, West Virginia, its hunger and fear, would be far behind me.

I got off in Charleston, searching for the way to my connecting train. I had only taken a few steps when I felt a hand grab my arm and smelled the citrus scent of Daniel's soap.

I pulled my arm away, and he reached forward and held me tight. I struggled to break free and stomped on his foot.

He pushed my face close to his and spoke through gritted teeth. "I'll tell them you robbed me. They'll find the rest of Abe's money on you, and you will go to jail."

I stopped struggling and looked beyond Daniel to see my train pulling out of the station. "How did you find me?"

"Your mother told me you were running away. I knew you wouldn't get far on foot. I saw Abe hand you the money and figured you'd go to the train station."

My mother was foolish enough to see the Cabots as benefactors.

***

I was silent on the train ride home. Daniel stared at me, his mouth twisted into a smirk. "You're hardly worth the trouble. Your bloom is fading, and you're getting fat."

He was ignorant as well as mean. I had nothing now, no family, no allies, just the hint of possibility in my womb that I was sure Daniel would take from me the minute he was born.

When I got home, I hugged Mama and smiled at Daddy. Let them think I was content to stay. I waited until the middle of the night to leave my bed and put on my black cloak. I touched the wall to say goodbye to Yeller.

***

The rope hung on a nail on the wall of the barn. It wasn't heavy. I made it to the oak before the moon had emerged from the clouds.

I climbed to a high branch. The face of the Cabot's house was silent. How surprised Daniel would be in the morning. How quickly word would spread among the neighbors. I'd seen my father hang pigs upside down to drain the blood plenty of times. I secured the rope, fashioned a noose, and placed it around my neck.

I imagined my body swaying in the wind, a spectral figure in my dark cloak. The bees would still buzz, the river would flood, girls would get visited in the night, and the Cabots would sit counting their money, polishing their silver, with no idea of what had been taken from them. I let myself fall.

Religion

My family have been members of the Slocum Baptist Church for four generations, but I never got religion until I went to the Lactation League meeting in Andersonville.

I was looking for the crafts club that meets in the community center, having recently taken up decoupage. It was a big deal for me. I'm not much of a joiner, but lately, I'd been feeling lonely, eager to make a change in my routine. I walked into a meeting room on the first floor and stood in the doorway. Eight chairs were arranged in a small circle. Women were standing in groups talking. A petite blonde woman waved me in.

"Please join us," she said. "You're right on time. I'm Caryn."

Before I could ask about crafts, the woman next to me cleared her throat and everyone took a seat.

"Hi, I'm Emily. Last time we met, I mentioned my desire to breastfeed my adopted baby. I'm happy to say that with a combination of blessed thistle, brewer's yeast, and fenugreek, along with pumping, I'm able to produce enough milk to breastfeed Rena."

The women applauded.

"Was there any nipple confusion?" asked Caryn.

"I finger fed Rena for the first few weeks, and last night she latched right on. I was so relieved."

That's when I noticed the babies sleeping in a row of carriers lined against the wall. I could barely see their faces as they were covered with caps and blankets. I decided to get up and leave. I stood and walked a few steps. Emily sprang to her feet and put her arms around me.

"Thanks for your support," she said, holding me against her enlarged breasts.

I hadn't been hugged like that in a long time. It would be rude to leave now. I returned to my seat.

"Bonding is so important," said a tall woman with close-cropped dark hair. "Ami is still on the breast at twenty-three months, and she is bright and engaged. I can tell it is as satisfying for her as it is for me."

My own breasts tingled. My face grew hot. I tried to imagine the feeling that would come from the intimacy of breastfeeding. Nothing could come close, not my parents tucking me in when I was a girl, not my awkward first kiss in the cloakroom in third grade, not holding my friend Jan when she lost her baby to a miscarriage. Suddenly decoupage seemed like a silly hobby.

I had never breastfed, never had any children. The only

time a guy had sucked my breasts was in high school. Bruce had broad shoulders and a crooked smile. He would play his guitar for me.

When my parents went out to the movies, he suggested that we hug lying down. We kissed and then he unbuttoned my shirt. He ran his hand over the top of my brassiere, and then he pulled the cup down and gently lifted my breast until the nipple showed. He lowered his head, gently kissed my nipple and then started to suck. I was nervous, numb even. I could hear him say, "Oh, baby" over and over again in a muffled declaration.

I looked around the circle. They were all looking at me.

"Hi, I'm Alice. I've been breastfeeding my son Sam since he was born. It is amazing. He looks at me with such trust, such love," I said, tears welling to my eyes. I was free of my small town life. No one had to know that I was a thirty-year-old virgin named Sandy or that I had driven here from Slocum to do crafts.

Emily came over and wrapped her arms around me.

When I got home, my house seemed so empty. I imagined the women from the club, each holding their baby close, the baby's small mouth latched onto her breast. What would it feel like to belong to someone so completely?

I work at Wilson and Meer as a bookkeeper. It's good steady work, no surprises. Sometimes I go out to lunch with the girls, but when the talk turns to husbands and children, I have nothing to contribute. They kid me about my freedom, no one to cook for or help with their homework.

I have women friends. I am a regular fixture at the church card parties, but lately, I look at other women's lives and wonder how I got here—alone in this quiet house with no one to keep me company.

I went up to my bedroom. The white crocheted bedcover looked inviting. My childhood teddy bear sat atop the bed. I took off my shoes and lay carefully across the bed, holding Teddy in my arms. I rocked slowly back and forth until I drifted off to sleep.

At our next meeting, the babies were wide awake. Celeste, the tall woman with short hair, made a play space for her daughter Ami in the corner with a set of blocks and a few books.

"You didn't bring Sam?" asked Caryn.

"He had a bit of a cold," I lied.

Emily held a gorgeous caramel-colored baby with big dark eyes. "Would you like to hold Rena?"

"Sure," I said, remembering someone talking about the need to support the baby's head. I looked into her eyes, holding her close against me; her head nestled in the crook of my arm.

No one blinked an eye when, in the middle of a discussion on breast pumps, Ami walked up to her mother and said, "Nursies!" Celeste put Ami on her lap, and Ami reached under her mother's shirt.

I fought the urge to laugh. When Ami laid her head against her mother's belly with a beatific look on her face, I felt chastened. The women around the circle mirrored the look on Ami's face as they watched Ami nursing.

I began to notice breasts all the time after that—and not just the big ones.

One afternoon during my lunch hour, I went to the maternity ward at the hospital and looked at the babies lined up in the window. They reminded me of kittens, sleeping with their eyes pressed closed, occasionally raising a fist in the air.

I went to the nurses' station, where a woman in a crisp uniform and cap greeted me.

"I was told I could get a breast pump here," I said.

"Fill out this form. There's a $10 deposit."

On the form, I gave the address of a house next to the community center. I waited until she brought out a small silver machine. "This is the Egnell SMB," said the nurse. "This silver piston causes the pump to suck and release. It's the best. My mom used to use a glass pump with a rubber ball attached, and it never got all her milk."

"Thank you," I said. "Thank you very much."

The Egnell looked a bit like a sewing machine with a hose and a pump. It was heavy in my arms. When I got home, I hid it under my bed. That night, I took it out. I slid my arm out of my flannel nightgown, exposing my breast. I put the pump up to my right breast and switched on the machine. The piston began to move, and I could feel the sucking.

It was loud. It didn't matter. I was alone. Max, my cat, died last year, and I never got another one. The pumping felt good. It felt like something I'd been born to do. I thought of Emily and her success at nursing. I pumped for fifteen minutes, but nothing came out.

The next day, my right breast was sore. I decided to alternate breasts. By the end of the week, I could barely stand the pressure of my blouse on my chest.

I went shopping for herbs at a store in Cincinnati. I went to the counter with my blessed thistle, brewer's yeast, and fenugreek.

"Trying to breastfeed?" asked the lady behind the counter with long gray hair and a flowing skirt of many colors.

"Yes," I said, lowering my eyes.

"None of my kids would take to it, no matter what I did. Don't let it make you feel less like a woman. There are a lot of ways to raise a child." She handed me my change and a small brown sack.

I took the herbs every day for weeks and continued to pump, but still, I was dry. I contemplated quitting the group. After all, how much longer could I make excuses for the absent baby? But World Breastfeeding Week was coming up, and I was supposed to run the information booth at the fairgrounds.

Friday night, I stopped by the grocery in Andersonville and ran into Celeste in the cereal aisle.

"Alice, is there any chance you could babysit for me tonight? My sitter has come down with a bad cold and I don't want to expose Ami to the germs."

"Sure. I'd be glad to."

"Great. Ami can finally meet Sam," said Celeste.

I felt my stomach drop. "Sam will be with my mother," I lied. "She can't get enough time with him."

I was on Celeste's doorstep at seven. She and her husband Jim were dressed for a nice dinner and a show. They brought me into the family room, where Ami was rolling a small truck across the floor. "This should keep her occupied for a while. When she gets hungry, I have some bottles in the fridge," said Celeste.

I stood in the doorway and waved as they drove off in their Chevy Impala. I went back to the couch and browsed the latest copy of *Life* magazine. After a while, Ami climbed up and sat beside me clutching a picture book. I placed her on my lap and read to her. As I read, she snuggled closer. When I finished the book, she nuzzled my chest and said "Nursies."

"Oh no, Ami. Aunt Alice has a bottle for you."

"Nursies," she said and began to cry.

Everything was quiet except for the sound of her crying. I reached up and began to unbutton my blouse.

Ami smiled and sniffed back her tears.

I pulled my right breast from the sling of my brassiere. My nipple grew tight and small in the open air. Ami bent her head and began to suck. I stroked her short, blond hair.

I felt my milk come in. Ami continued to suck contentedly.

"Oh, sweet baby," I said softly. I felt myself flush. I held her close and imagined this was my house. That Jim turned to me at night and lifted my nightgown. That Ami joined us in bed each morning to nurse.

When Ami was done nursing, I went into the kitchen and poured a bottle of milk down the drain. This must be what shoplifting feels like, taking something that isn't yours and hoping that no one would find out.

I returned the pump, got my ten-dollar deposit back. Though it was tempting, I never returned to the lactation group. Instead, I joined a decoupage group that met in Eve Hunter's basement in Slocum every Saturday morning. Sometimes, when I am cutting and pasting pictures, I feel a familiar pang of loneliness and think of the women sitting in a circle, the sun shining through the window, the babies' small mouths sucking away, so hungry.

Harvest

When she turned seventy, Abby Linder removed all the mirrors from her house. It wasn't enough to cover them. She didn't want to have to explain herself to visitors. It was better to take them away. Even so, she couldn't escape her reflection.

She'd been on the bus in Lexington. It was a sunny day, and the faces of the riders reflected in the window. She examined each of them. The young mother with tired eyes and pudgy cheeks leaned against the window. The handsome man in overalls had a faraway look in his eyes. The old crone with a face that had grown square with age looked vaguely familiar. She raised her hand to her mouth at exactly the same time Abby did. The woman in the glass shuddered and turned away.

Abby even took down the mirror on the wall of Goodies Candy Store, which she had owned for 40 years. The store was an institution, one of the longest-running businesses in Slocum.

A student from Slocum High School, David Emerson, painted a mural in its place. She told him to use his imagination. In the scene, lollipops hung from trees; the clouds were shaped like marshmallows, and a river of chocolate flowed through town.

David had delicate features and long fingers. While he painted, Abby sat behind the counter sucking on lemon drops and watching him work, imagining his young skin, soft and smooth under his chaste white button-down shirt. This made her feel alive.

After a few hours, he asked for a drink. She brought him sweet tea.

"This is good," he said. He sat in a folding chair and surveyed his work. "Do you like it?"

In the mural, children bent down by the river lapping up the chocolate like dogs. She didn't much like it, children behaving like animals, but it was better than seeing herself in the mirror.

"It's wonderful," she said. "You have a real gift."

David stayed seated and looked around the room. "When did you know you wanted to sell candy?"

"I just kind of stumbled into it," she said. "I never imagined my life like this."

What did you think you'd do?" he asked.

"I guess be a mother, raise a family," said Abby. There had been proposals, of course, just never at the right time or from the right man.

They sat silently while he finished his tea.

"I better get home," David said. "I have homework."

He set the sweaty glass on the counter and left.

A handful of folks in town would remember that Abby was once homecoming queen, sitting in a convertible, the top down, a bouquet of roses in her lap. It was a big deal in a small town. Her hair had been black and silky, her skin firm and flawless.

She'd felt wonderful in the pink satin gown.

That night, she lost her virginity in the front seat of the car to a solid boy with short hair whose nickname was "Tank." His sole virtue was that he had the courage to ask her to the dance.

She wasn't sure why she slept with him. Maybe she was grateful he took her to the dance. As he moved in and out of her, he said *thanks* over and over again with a slight lisp. She would remember him as "Tanks" and was skeptical of overly appreciative lovers after that.

Abby found the roses while cleaning out the car the next day, their delicate petals crushed by the thrashing about. She threw them in the trash.

Back then, Abby used her beauty to get noticed. Everyone watched her when she walked by. She practiced her walk alone in her room with the door closed. Abby had no problem getting a job at Deem's Berry Farm. For years, men stopped to change her flat tire and offered to carry her groceries. Now she was invisible unless she was standing behind the candy counter.

The bell attached to the door of the candy store rang nonstop around 2:30 when the kids from Slocum Elementary came in for penny candy. Adam Lang dumped handfuls of Zotz and Pixy Sticks on the counter.

"That will be 25 cents, sir," said Abby.

Adam handed her a quarter.

Sheila Bell had a candy necklace, candy cigarettes, and an open pack of Now & Laters. Abby looked at the Now & Laters in mock horror. "We must have a problem with mice," she said.

Sheila giggled.

When the children left, Abby locked the door, flipped the sign, and went to sit in the storeroom. It was quiet and dark, and the tidy rows of boxes comforted her. She thought about the photographer who had been by that morning when she was decorating the front window. He introduced himself politely and said something about a bicentennial project. She imagined the photo, herself looking wrinkled and spindly among the streamers and giant lollipops in the window. She sent him away.

After fifteen minutes, she went back out front, unlocked the door, and flipped the sign. There would be other customers, teenagers buying candy bars full of nuts and nougat, women buying dark chocolate toffee, and Wally from the barbershop stopping in for his usual bag of circus peanuts.

That evening, after a simple supper of tomato soup and a chicken salad sandwich, Abby settled in front of the television with a box of colored pipe cleaners and a pair of scissors. Accompanied by the drone of the television, she twisted the wires into small shapes, a bumblebee, a dachshund, a giraffe, and a lady bug. She added them to a shoebox that was nearly full.

On Sundays, Abby visited Tony Conti in the nursing home. She and Tony had gone to school together and had the same afterschool job picking berries at Deem's Berry Farm.

They had worked side by side talking as they slipped berries, still warm from the sun, into their mouths. Once, when a bee stung her, he removed the stinger and placed her finger in his mouth to suck out the venom. She laughed and pushed him away, but never forgot the way he looked, his lips around her finger, his eyes closed, his long, dark lashes beautiful in the sunlight.

When she looked at him now, she still saw the tall boy with the baby face and black curls, who blushed easily, not an old man with a grizzled beard who sometimes forgot his own name, but could still sing the high school anthem.

Sometimes she wished she had a picture of him back then—his young face, those deep brown eyes, but she preferred the memory of the way the sun felt on her face and the warmth of his lips on her finger.

They had never been romantic, but once she had felt him lean forward and smell her hair when he thought she wasn't looking. She had wanted him too, but he was so open, so sweet, she didn't want to break his heart.

When she walked into his room, Tony was looking out the window of his small room at a bird feeder where a yellow finch perched.

"Hello, Tony." said Abby.

He turned to face her, and a look of recognition crossed his face. A good day.

"I brought you something." She pulled a small red berry made of pipe cleaner from her bag and placed it in his palm.

"Deem's," he said. "Imagine what berry picking would do to us now."

They sat on his twin bed. The only personal touch in the room was a double wedding ring pattern quilt that Abby had bought secondhand.

"How is Sammy?" he asked. Abby's dog Sammy had been dead for ten years.

"Fine," said Abby.

She knew better than to ask after Tony's ex-wives. Gina had been beautiful and mean. She left Tony when she decided that he'd never make enough money making furniture. Allison had been kinder, but flighty. The rumor was that she left town with Miss Campbell, the school counselor, that they were lovers.

He turned to face her. She reached out and took his hands.

"How are you, Tony?"

"I'm doing all right. I was trying to remember that song we used to sing while we picked."

"I Wanna Be Loved by You?"

"That's it."

"I wanna be loved by you."

"Just you," he said.

"Nobody else but you," she answered.

"I wanna be loved by you—alone. Boo boo bee doo," they sang together.

"I miss you." She kissed the top of his head.

I miss you too," he echoed, uncertainly.

***

The years had slipped away, and the person she had been disappeared with them, replaced by an old woman with wrinkles and bifocals, who men opened doors for or offered a hand up but nothing more.

For years, Abby had kept company with Charlie Jones, a beekeeper with a farm outside Slocum. They would go out to dinner in Andersonville and come back to her place to watch television, and at a certain point in the night, he would lean over and whisper in her ear, inviting her into the bedroom.

Abby bought lingerie for the occasion and would spend the day thinking about the delicate silk panties that she wore under her black A-line skirt, the coffee-colored lace bra under her crew neck sweater.

Charlie died of a heart attack at 45. Now she wore plain cotton panties and slept in a t-shirt her nephew had given her with a picture of Charlie Chaplin on the front. She had never planned to be obsolete.

Abby had her routines, the candy store, her hobbies, a weekly card party on Thursday night, church and visiting Tony on Sunday afternoons.

She walked the six blocks to church for the card party

each Thursday. This week, she carried a shoebox full of her animals for the church bazaar. She had several blocks to go when she heard the sound of bikes behind her. The boys liked to get up speed and jump off the curbs, momentarily taking flight. One boy whizzed past her on the right. Another on the left. A third was so close that he banged into her arm.

Everything slowed down as she felt herself falling. Her shoebox flew from her hands. She put out her arms to break her fall and ended up sitting on the pavement with bloody palms, her small creations scattered around her.

The boy looked back. It was David Emerson. She raised her hand in greeting and could see him hesitate and then turn away.

"Aren't you going to help your girlfriend?" one of the boys asked.

David paused and then rode off.

Abby sat on the pavement, tears of frustration springing to her eyes. She drew the shoebox close and picked up each of her animals, placing them in the box with care. Willing herself not to cry, she got slowly to her feet and continued the journey to church.

When she got there, the ladies cooed over her wounds. Sandy spread salve over her palms.

"When you get old, it's like you're invisible," she warned her friends.

"Those kids ought to pay more attention," said Julie.

"Thank God you didn't break a bone," said Jan.

The women brought her cake and coffee. Though Abby wasn't sure, it seemed as if they let her win at gin rummy. The winner got to take the rest of the cake home, so she didn't protest.

The next day, Abby was sore and had a bruise on her elbow. She sat at the counter staring at a bin full of brightly colored jellybeans. The bell rang, and she glanced at the door. David Emerson had come to get paid. He was holding a bouquet of daisies.

"I'm sorry," he said, holding out the flowers.

"Apology accepted," she said, exchanging the flowers for his pay envelope.

He looked at Abby and then his mural. "The perspective is a little off," he said.

"Yes," she said. "Yes it is."

That evening, she went to see Tony.

When Abby got to Tony's room, he was staring at himself in the mirror over the vanity with a look of concern. "Who is that old guy?" he asked.

"It's you Tony," said Abby. "Still you." She stood behind him, their faces reflected in the mirror. "What is it?" she put her hand on his shoulder.

"I'm trying to remember what it felt like to be young," he said, and a tear rolled down his cheeks.

She put her arms around him and turned him until he was facing her.

"I can't remember a thing about what it felt like," he said.

She looked at his room. It could have been anywhere, a hotel room or the nondescript bedroom of a grown child, but it was the nursing home where Tony would die alone. She held him closer.

"It feels like this," said Abby. She took his hand, rough with years of manual labor, spotted with age. She brought it to her lips, slowly kissing every finger and then his palms. She slipped his forefinger into her mouth as he had done for her so many years ago when she got stung.

She realized then that she still felt like that sixteen-year-old, no matter how much time had passed. His breathing slowed, and he rested his head on her shoulder. She thought of them together, warmed by the sun, their heads bent over a field of slowly ripening berries.

Life After

Jacob's wasn't the first death at Quarryside. He joined the lore of the soldier just back from World War Two, who snuck into the quarry at night and suffered a cramp so bad that he couldn't save himself, and the tragic story of a baby girl named Adele, who fell face down in a corner of the baby pool while her mother chatted up the lifeguard. The stories were meant to be cautionary tales, but they didn't change a thing. My boy was gone.

I kept thinking of my swollen belly and the way I had winced anytime Sam stopped short when we were in the car and, later, the way I cradled Jacob's head when he slept in my arms. I'd watched Jacob grow strong and tall. I'd run after him holding out his bike helmet. I'd watched him drive off in a two-ton car, hoping he wouldn't hit anything. I hadn't worried about the pool. Jacob had always been a strong swimmer.

The coroner said Jacob died instantly, a combination of the force of his dive and the angle at which his head hit the bottom of the quarry. His skull was cracked, his neck broken. Sam insisted that I not see him that way. He identified the body, so Jacob remained whole in my mind, his long hair swept to the side, his skin golden as if he'd been dipped in sunshine, a small smattering of freckles on his cheeks. His now mannish body tall and strong. But Jacob was gone, disappeared. No amount of mental conjuring would bring him back, and when I saw him in my dreams, he never spoke, not a word.

I used to think about the families of children who were abducted, the excruciating tension they must feel waking up every day and wondering if this would be the day they would see their child again. I would have found that nightmare, that agonizing hope, preferable to the creeping numbness that had taken over my life.

Everyone was so nice, even people who had no interest in me before. Our society has a special fondness for women who suffer, especially when their suffering is public. I got dinner invitations from the well-connected moms looking for some kind of project. Tragedy vampires. I imagined them choosing between me and the library book sale or the orchestra gala. I'd smile and say, "I'm busy, but we must get together soon."

I went through the motions. Three days a week, I'd meet my friend Ann at Quarryside to water walk, just as we had before Jacob died. This got me out of the house and moving. Without it, I might have spent all day in bed, my body weighed down with grief. The sun shone on the water, and children shouted as they jumped off the diving board. Life went on as if nothing happened.

It was strangely calming to listen to Ann talk about her life. She complained about the profanity and sex scenes on whatever series she was following on Netflix. I imagined her astride her exercise bike watching the sex scenes over and over, pedaling harder as the woman on screen whimpered. She talked endlessly about an old tree that was being taken down in her backyard. A tree for fuck's sake, as if it were a real loss. It was all I could do not to dig my nails into her flesh to see the crescents of blood rise. I found myself digging my fingernails into my own palms instead.

I had to make an effort to see the spot where the accident happened. It was where the water started to get deep. Jacob had hit a slope of concrete right before the drop off. I made myself look in that direction every day. I thought of it as bearing witness. Were there traces of Jacob's blood in the water? Though I dreaded it, I made myself go back to the pool. The only way I could survive the loss was to face it head on, and the longer I waited, the more it would haunt me. I waited two months and went on a Monday morning when I hoped it would be less crowded. My first time back in the water, I'd felt the urge to swallow a mouthful. Then I wondered if the chlorine had removed every evidence of him.

When Jacob was a baby, I brought him to the baby pool and placed him in a special float that showed him off like a child emperor. He was chubby and happy. I was proud when he smiled at passersby. I took delight when he laughed.

My attention shifted when I had Jacob. Suddenly, everything else took a back seat, including my relationship with Sam. It seemed so cliché, but it was true. My connection to Jacob was so elemental, so physical, that I had little desire for anything else.

We had passed the six weeks of healing my obstetrician recommended before having sex when Sam turned to me in bed one night.

"Hi," he said. His voice was husky. This was a game we had played when we were newly married, pretending we had just met.

"Hi. Are you new here?"

Sam started at my forehead, kissing me lightly there and then on each closed eyelid, the end of my nose and then deeply on the mouth, with a hunger that I didn't remember from our other encounters. He took his time making his way down my body, and as he did, he brought me back into myself.

I was grateful, as if he had saved me from some mysterious siren call, the baby ready to lure me to danger with his chubby cheeks and long eyelashes. Still, as soon as we were done, I went in to check on Jacob and spent a long time staring down at him, marveling at what we had made.

Later, Sam and I made eye contact when Jacob scored a soccer goal and held hands when he received his high school diploma. Jacob was our collaboration, and without him, we were lost to each other.

Jacob had been home for the summer before starting his third year in animation at Pratt. He spent mornings in his room glued to his computer screen, afternoons at the pool, and evenings out at the bar with his best friend Ethan, who'd stayed close to home to attend the University of Connecticut. I had just gotten used to this adult version of Jacob, who would still leave his clothes on his bedroom floor, but who would thank me for dinner, telling me how much he had enjoyed the shrimp stir-fry. Then he was gone.

Jacob's funeral was packed with his friends. Young men in dark suits, the chubby cheeks of childhood replaced with beards. Impossibly beautiful young women in low-cut black dresses and heels. These kids were so polished, their hair so shiny and teeth so white, it was as if they all employed stylists. After the service, I saw Ethan in the corner looking at photos of Jacob, tears running down his face. I stood beside him, and he put his arm around my shoulder and gave me a smile that I could only describe as brave. Sweet Ethan. I understood why Jacob picked him for his best friend.

Grief separated Sam and me. The night of the funeral, I sat on the end of our bed and cried. I expected Sam to put his arm around me. He touched my shoulder and then left the room. I heard the television go on downstairs. I crawled into bed and hugged my pillow.

Sam worked late, and when he was home, he would sit on the couch changing the channel or moving between the newspaper and a book, unable to settle his mind.

One evening, I sat on the arm of his chair. "Do you mind if I sit here? I don't know anyone at this party?"

Sam looked at me angrily. "Too soon, Beth."

I was looking for a way to wake myself up and to draw Sam out of his doldrums. After the death of our parents, we had taken solace in each other with a ferocity and frequency that surpassed even our courting days. It was as if sex could ward off death, each orgasm not a little death, but some kind of tiny birth.

His rejection stung. I went upstairs, stopping in front of Jacob's door, placing my palm on the cold wood. I opened the door and slid inside, keeping the lights off. I sat on the edge of Jacob's bed, my eyes slowly adjusting to the dark. I could see shadows of trophies on a shelf along the wall, a pile of clothes in the corner. I lay back on the bed and wept. I woke up with the sun peeking through the shade. The house was empty.

It didn't seem strange when Ethan showed up one afternoon. I had noticed him driving by when I was out front pulling up weeds. I invited him in.

"Would you like something to drink?"

"Do you have any beer?"

I handed him an orange soda, Jacob's favorite.

I tried to imagine what Jacob's death was like for him. It was probably an unwelcome reminder of mortality in a time when you were supposed to feel invincible. It wasn't about mortality for me. It was more like surviving nuclear war, where everything you knew, everything you saw, was unalterably changed, and you wondered if you wanted to live in this barren, burned-out version of the world.

"How are you doing?" he asked.

I was supposed to be the grownup, and he was asking me.

"Okay." I lied. "How are you, Ethan?"

"I can't sleep. I keep crying at strange times."

"I'm so sorry. So sorry." I placed my hand on his cheek, tears welling up in my eyes.

Ethan had grown tall, almost six feet. His shoulders had broadened, and his face had transformed from cute to handsome. Even his hands, holding that orange soda, were the hands of a man, not a boy.

I felt a sudden awkwardness around him that reminded me of high school when one of the football players said "hello" in the hallway. This was nonsense. I had known this kid forever. He was Jacob's best friend. This was just my mind's way of diverting my attention from my grief.

"It's like he just disappeared off the face of the Earth," said Ethan. His mouth quivered.

"I know," I said. I patted his shoulder. "It won't always feel like this," I said, though that was a lie. I was sure my grief would never lift.

Ethan returned the next week with a bouquet of yellow roses. He held them like they were breakable. "Thanks for being so nice."

"Anytime," I said.

I noticed Ethan glancing up the stairs.

"Would you like to hang out in Jacob's room?"

"Sure."

He seemed tentative.

"Really, it's not a problem. I go in there myself sometimes."

I could see Ethan relax. He went slowly up the stairs.

I went into the kitchen and started the dishes. I could hear the television come on and the sound of *Dragon War,* Jacob's favorite video game. I felt my heart constrict. I let myself imagine it was Jacob up there.

Ethan played for hours and came downstairs bleary-eyed.

"Feel any better?"

"A little bit," he said. "How are you?"

"I'm taking it minute by minute."

He smiled when he saw the roses that I'd put in a vase on the table.

"So thoughtful of you," I said. He waved away my compliment and walked out the door.

The house felt especially quiet with Ethan gone. I went up to Jacob's room. It smelled like a combination of sweat and aftershave. I breathed it in.

I picked up the controller, which looked like something out of a science fiction movie. There were buttons marked by numbers and a button to press to start the game and something that looked like a plus sign that could move the player in all directions.

I turned on the game and pressed start. A muscular figure showed up on the screen followed by a map that showed the location of a damsel in distress. I hit a button, and my character made his way through the forest. I didn't get far before a dragon appeared. I pressed the buttons frantically while the dragon breathed fire on my character, and he crumpled to the ground. Slowly, I caught on.

The next time Ethan came by, I asked if I could play too. We played for two hours, and by the end of the afternoon, I learned when to release which potion and how to use my bow and arrow to slay the dragon. I caught myself looking at Ethan's broad shoulders and muscular arms.

Grief makes people crazy, I thought to myself.

That night, I felt lighter. I made dinner and set the table, hoping that a sit-down meal might spur some conversation, some connection between Sam and me. Sam came in at 6:30 and headed for his recliner.

"I thought we could," I gestured towards the table.

"It looks nice, Beth." He summoned a smile.

We sat. I passed the salad bowl. "How was your day?"

"Nothing special. I got the brand analysis ready for tomorrow's meeting. You?"

"I played video games," I said. I tried to hide the slight thrill it gave me to admit it. I was ashamed that it was the one thing that made me feel closer to Jacob, not the pictures, not videos of family vacations, just some stupid game where I got to kill dragons.

Sam looked at me out of the corner of his eyes. "That's nice."

No questions about why or with who or what it felt like. I focused on my plate and felt the silence fill up the space between us.

After dinner, I left Sam to his television and went for a walk. The air was cool on my skin. Gold, red, and deep brown leaves fell slowly to the ground. I passed illuminated windows that held dioramas of families around tables eating, talking, and laughing. I wanted to knock on their doors and warn them that it wouldn't always be like this. People would die or go away or retreat into themselves. Their lives would be forever altered, and they'd have no choice but to try to forge new ones and fill those empty spaces.

Ethan didn't show up the next week. I was starting to give up hope that I would see him again when he showed up late one afternoon with a six-pack of beer. He raised his eyebrows at me, and I laughed and waved him inside.

We settled on the floor, our backs against the bed, knees up, the controllers in our hands. I thought back to my father yelling at me not to sit too close to the television.

Ethan opened a beer and tilted it my way. I took it, feeling the cool glass of the bottle on my hand. I took a swig and set the beer next to me on the floor. I didn't ask if it was Jacob's favorite.

I got lost in the game, tracking through the woods, plunging my sword into a dragon, shooting arrows at evil elves. It was a world where things made sense, and justice was as easy as a clean shot. My whole body was engaged. I'd made it to level three when we took a break.

"You're good. Are you sure you haven't played before?"

"You don't need to lie to the old lady," I said. I tilted my head back and finished my beer.

"You're not…"

"I'll get some snacks." As I walked out, I saw Ethan's reflection in the mirror as he watched my backside. I grew warm in a way that I'd forgotten. I found bags of chips and popcorn and a few bottles of water.

When I sat down, Ethan handed me another beer. I took it and handed him the chips. We ate in silence. I downed the beer and started to feel buzzed. Ethan turned the game back on, and I ventured into level four.

I fought elves that came out of nowhere, shot a golden phoenix and got extra life points, and masterfully fought a dragon by getting too close to get burned and plunging a knife into its breastbone.

"Damn fine play!" said Ethan.

"Right?" I said. I fell over sideways, laughing at my hidden prowess. I lay on my back trying to get my breath. Ethan leaned over me laughing, his face coming closer, his lips parting.

I wanted that kiss. I wanted to be someone besides the grieving mother. I wanted to forget my loss and blow up my life, which felt so heavy and sad.

I thought about what it could be like to fuck him. Would it be some kind of reverse birth, taking this young man inside me, letting him fill my empty places? I knew that if I thought about it in the right way, I could convince myself that fucking him was an act of healing, for him and for me.

"Oh, Ethan." I turned my head to the side. His lips

brushed my cheek, and he sat upright. I sat up and turned to face him. "Sometimes people go a little crazy when they're grieving. I've read books that say don't make any major life decisions for a year—no selling my house, or changing jobs. No kissing you."

He blushed and looked down at his hands, which still held the controller. "I better go."

We stood.

"Take this."

I took a picture of Jacob and Ethan off Jacob's dresser. They were twelve, just starting to get tall. They were arm in arm, staring at the camera with a look of such confidence and hope.

Ethan looked at it then tucked it carefully in his shirt pocket.

***

Sam got home at six. I sat on the living room sofa. He sat in his chair. It was bare—no paper or books nearby, no channel changer. I had hidden those away.

"What's up?" he asked.

I stayed silent.

"What is it, Beth?"

"He's gone, Sam. He won't be coming back. I need you here with me."

"I know," he said, his voice breaking.

"I need you here with me," I repeated.

He got up and joined me on the sofa.

Outside, dusk was falling, and families were sitting down to dinner. Mothers were putting babies to bed. Young people were making plans for later that night.

Inside our house, it was quiet. Sam was holding my hand as he leaned close. "What happens now?" he asked.

"I don't know."

I held him tight as silence surrounded us.

After the Fall

I was born Charlotte Grisham, but after Adam and I broke up, I changed my name to Eve. It seemed fitting; after all, I was making a fresh start. Adam and I had dated since birth, well, actually just since high school; it just felt like forever.

He broke up with me after he failed a quiz in a women's magazine. *Who is smarter, you or your mate?* He scored 15 points lower than me, landing him in the "Get a Clue" section of the score sheet.

I told him it was just a magazine quiz, but I knew I was smarter than he was and that he'd be happier with another girl. I didn't stop him when he packed his bags and headed out the door.

After the break-up, I decided to move from Indiana to Washington State. I heard it was beautiful, real untouched country. I wanted to a change of scenery. Every place, including the dry cleaners, reminded me of Adam.

I got off the plane, bought a junker of a car, and drove across the state. That's how I ended up at Grimaldi Gardens.

It was part apple orchard, part winery. They needed someone who could fill in wherever they needed help.

Some days I'd pick apples next to a couple of migrant workers. I loved it. The guys were friendly and didn't mind my patchwork high school Spanish. We'd eat lunch together, and they'd cut off small bits of tamale for me to sample, each vying for my approval. Manuel's tortillas were full of soft white cheese and a salsa that was slightly sweet. Romero's were spicy with a really hot finish. I gave them both thumbs up, and they seemed happy.

Other times, I'd handpick grapes or help pour the juice into barrels. That was a two-person job, so I had to work with Tony Grimaldi, the farm manager.

Tony was handsome in a dangerous way–deep-set eyes, a weathered face, and hair made the color of caramel by the sun. He wore a heavy gold cross around his neck and a thick, silver wedding ring. When he was working out a problem on the farm, Tony would twist his ring over and over so fast that it was hard to look away. He had a way of staring right through me that took my breath away.

It took a few weeks, but after a while, I started to feel like I really fit in. The farm was my world now. I woke up to the sound of the birds in the morning and fell asleep to the sound of crickets.

At lunch, I'd bring grapes to the orchard for Manuel and Romero. They'd smile and open their mouths playfully as I tried to toss a grape inside. I'd take turns, feeding one and then the other, and save the last bunch for myself. Once I caught Tony staring at us, fingering his cross absently.

His brother Jerome said, "Don't mind Tony. He hasn't been the same since Rosa left." Rosa was his wife. She'd taken off with one of the workers in the middle of the night, leaving only her wedding ring behind.

Tony was moody, but the rest of the Grimaldis were wonderful. On Sundays, they would set up long tables in the orchard and serve the crew fried chicken, potato salad, and apple pie. I'd sit between Manuel and Romero and teach them the names of the food. I showed them how to pick the crunchy skin off the bottom of the pieces of chicken until they were picked clean. I made sure they got slices of cheddar cheese for their pie.

One of the few women on the crew, I stayed with the others in a small cottage on the edge of the orchard. At night when I couldn't sleep I'd walk through the trees, protected by their canopy. I loved to look for moonlight through the branches.

It was cloudy the night I ran into Tony. He was sitting against the tree we'd marked for harvest the next day. I could smell the ripening apples in the air.

"Nice night. Are you out for a walk?" I asked, knowing his answer.

"I've seen you walking. I knew you'd be here," he replied.

"Was there something you wanted to talk about?" I asked.

His voice was thick with emotion. "You and those migrant workers, it just ain't right."

"They are my friends, nothing more."

"You've got a lot to learn, girl. There is always something more," said Tony.

The clouds parted. I could see his eyes burning as he looked up at me. I fought the urge to run, as his hands grasped my wrists and pulled me down to the grass.

"Don't you get it? There is always something more."

He started to shake me, his back falling against the tree. I was afraid of what would come next. As he shook me, apples landed on the ground around us. Tony reached for one and pressed it to my lips.

"Taste it!" he said, through gritted teeth. "Take a bite." He pushed it into my hands and brought my hands to my mouth.

I closed my eyes and took a bite, choking on the skin and pulp, forcing myself to swallow. When I opened my eyes, Tony's eyes were fixed on his ring. Tears ran down his face as he twisted it in circles. I got up quietly, ran back to the cottage, and locked the door.

The next morning, there were bruises on my wrists and two new workers in the orchard, white boys from down South.

After I packed up my stuff, I went down to the orchard and picked up the apples that had fallen the night before.

I ate the apples as I drove down the highway. They had a bruised, bitter taste. I threw the cores out the window and watched in my rearview as they splintered on the pavement.

A Rumor of Fire

Rumors traveled quickly in the Westlake Apartment complex. Mrs. Orton was a drinker. It was an open secret that baby Olivia, whom we all visited and cooed over, wasn't Andrea Coster's. She was too old to have a baby. Olivia was the product of an affair her husband had with a younger woman who was on drugs and couldn't care for the child.

Everyone said Cindy, who wore the black bikini and slathered herself with baby oil, had slept with the handsome maintenance man with sleepy eyes, even though he had a son with gorgeous curls and a skinny wife who always seemed to be looking at the sky. Still, I'd borrow Cindy's baby oil thinking it might make me sexy like her, though I was what my mother called "a late bloomer."

Dad told me not to "traffic in gossip."

"Keep your own counsel," he said, whatever that meant. Dad was smart and funny and always listened when I talked.

But, the rumor of a fire in the laundry room was definitely true. Me and my friend Charmaine went to see the burn marks on the walls and could smell the lingering smoke. Management replaced the old dinged up dryer with a new one that had a window in the front so you could watch the clothes toss around. They also installed a fire alarm on the wall.

Charmaine and I thought of ourselves as the unofficial detectives of the complex. We were a great team, like Sony and Cher or Pink Lady and Jeff (though they are really a trio). We called each other at night and talk on the phone while we're watching TV. One time, I said Dolly Parton looked fat in her jumpsuit, and Charmaine swore she was about to say the same thing. We had spent all of last summer following the comings and goings of the Donatella Brothers delivery truck. We were sure they were drug dealers, though we only saw them drop off fruit baskets.

The firemen said it was faulty wiring on the dryer, but we were sure it was arson. It happened all the time in those cop shows. My dad had studied philosophy in school but became a cop, which was what I've wanted to be since I was young enough to sport a plastic badge.

Dad once helped stop a robbery. He came home that night and said, "All human failings are because of love or money or love of money." Mom rolled her eyes.

I thought about the fire before I fell asleep and wondered what happened to the clothes in the dryer. I imagined nylon panties melted into little blobs, a baby blanket ignited, and a white cotton blouse turned black. Dark, I know. I read about teen angst in my mother's magazine. The article said everything is all sex and blackness and hell fire in the songs and books for kids my age. The article said that it was all a substitute for ancient coming-of-age rituals. A noted psychologist said that turning up Led Zeppelin on the car radio helps kids take the edge off.

Charmaine and I figured it was our job to find out what had really happened during the fire. We started by staking out the laundry room. Charmaine sat outside on the stairs pretending to read a book. She had her mother's meditation gong in her pocket. I hung around in the utility closet of the laundry room. It was dark and warm in the closet. The air had that warm dryer smell that was so comforting in the wintertime. I tried to imagine it was cold outside, as sweat dripped down my back.

The laundry room door was propped open, and I listened for the gong, which signaled someone heading for the laundry room. I heard the gong and then Charmaine's voice going "ohm" over and over. I almost cracked up.

I peeked through the door and saw Clint Dahlem, who we secretly called "mustache Joe," come in with a basketful of gray towels and gray sweat socks. Clint was humming the guitar part from In-A-Gadda-Da-Vida and doing a surprisingly decent job of it. He loaded up the machines with quarters. He was dropping handfuls of socks and underwear into the machine when I saw him lift an old sweat sock to his nose and smell it. He made a face, but was kind of smiling like he liked it. My stomach turned. Gross. What a skeez.

Clint left, and I waited a few minutes before joining Charmaine on the landing. After the hot air in the laundry room, the breeze was wonderful.

"Nothing yet." I said.

"This may take time."

"No, duh."

"No, duh."

"Stop mocking me."

"You stop."

We broke up laughing.

"You take a turn in the laundry room."

"But it's my mother's gong," she said.

"Weak excuse."

We'd decided to spend the night in the laundry room and see who showed up. I told my mother I was at Charmaine's house, and she told her mother she was at my house.

We each grabbed our sleeping bags on the way out and some snacks. Our sleeping bags blanketed the floor of the utility closet. We spread out our snacks – Cheetos and King Dons and Charleston Chews. I crept out and got us sodas from the vending machine. If we had to go to the bathroom, we could use the locker room by the pool. We had everything covered, or so we thought.

Charmaine brought a deck of cards, and we played Rummy and Go Fish using hand signals rather than words in case anyone came in. Around 9:30, we heard the door to the laundry room creak open. We peeked through a crack in the door. It was

Johnny Cutler. He was new to the complex. It was just him and his mom in their apartment, and she was gone all the time working double shifts as a nurse. He was around our age, thirteen, but he had the slightest shade of a mustache and a hand-tooled leather wallet chained to his belt loop. He was kind of greasy, but kind of sexy. My mom said he "looked like trouble."

Charmaine said he was gross, but she smiled too much when she said it, so I knew she liked him too.

Johnny didn't have any laundry with him. He reached into his pocket and pulled out a handful of quarters. He put the change in the vending machine, and a bag of chips slowly pushed forward on a coil. "Funions," mouthed Charmaine. She loved Funions, and I was pretty sure she thought this was a cosmic sign that Johnny was meant for her.

Charmaine had hair like the girl on the Breck commercial, shiny and bouncy. She didn't wear braces. She had been an "early bloomer." Sometimes I was jealous of her, but then I thought of her father, who seemed never to have time for her, and I felt better.

The Funions hung at the end of the coil without dropping. "Damn," Johnny cursed. He banged on the front of the machine with his fists, and the Funions didn't move.

"God damn, mother fucking..."

Charmaine looked like she was about to burst out laughing. I pinched my arm to keep a straight face.

Then Johnny backed up and kicked the machine hard, over and over. It rocked back and forth.

"You bastard," he said. "You deadbeat. Just taking off. The hell with me and mom."

We watched as the machine swayed. The Funions fell and plenty of other snacks too. Finally, Johnny stopped kicking. He wiped his face on the edge of his Iron Maiden t-shirt and grabbed the Funions and a couple of candy bars and left.

Charmaine ran out and grabbed the candy left in the bottom of the machine. We split it, neither of us mentioning Johnny's tears. We knew tons of kids whose parents were divorced. We both agreed we couldn't stand it if our parents split up.

"I would just die," I said.

"Curl up and die," echoed Charmaine.

I hated to think it, but her folks would probably be more likely to split. They argued all the time, like it was a game or something. My folks never argued. The only way I knew they disagreed was when my mom's mouth made a tight, straight line.

We continued our card game, and about an hour later, we heard the door creak again. We peeked out the door and saw Joe and Sue Collins, an older couple, come in carrying a portable tape player.

"Nice and quiet. I told you," said Sue.

Joe nodded as he pushed the laundry table against the wall. Sue placed the tape player on the table and pressed play. Old-timey music filled the room. Sue stood in the middle of the room, her arms out. Joe took her hand, and they began to dance, stepping back and forth in time, as if they'd done it a million times before.

"Isn't this better?" he asked. "We have room to move around here."

"Remember the Crystal ballroom? The way we glided across that floor?"

"Yes. We do alright," he said and kissed her.

I mouthed "sweet" to Charmaine. She puckered her mouth until she had a fish face. I elbowed her until she stopped. We watched as they danced for thirty minutes. When they were done, they sat in folding chairs facing one another. Joe lifted Sue's foot and took off her high heels. He rubbed her toes gently, while he hummed. After a while, he helped her back on with her shoes. Joe held the tape player with one hand and held Sue's hand with the other as they left.

So far we were getting nowhere with the investigation. We had Johnny on property damage if we wanted to turn him in, but what's a few candy bars compared to a deadbeat dad. It was getting close to midnight, and Charmaine's eyes were drooping when we heard the laundry room door open. It was bikini Cindy with a small basketful of silky things.

I made a face. Charmaine crossed her eyes. Cindy set the washer on delicate and poured in some Woolite. While the washer began to fill, Cindy stood in the middle of the floor and bent her head until her hair fell forward. She fluffed it from underneath and then flipped her hair back.

She was expecting someone, maybe the person who set the fire. Then I saw my father walk through the door. He walked right over to Cindy and kissed her on the lips.

"You look so hot you could start a fire," he said.

I stepped further back into the closet. Charmaine watched. From the look on her face, they must have kissed. I looked away but felt her squeeze my hand. I turned to her in time to see Charmaine lean out of the closet and pull the fire alarm on the wall.

My father and Cindy left so quickly that she left her laundry behind. Charmaine grabbed the basket as we ran from the building. We went to hide in the woods behind the apartments. We could see the flashing lights of the fire engine. The firemen were too busy looking for a blaze to notice the small fire we made in a clearing.

Charmaine found matches in her purse, along with a small bag of sunflower seeds. We made a clear space in the dirt, and I built a small pyramid with the clothes. The pointed cup of Cindy's brassiere lay on top. It made me sick to look at it and wonder if my father had touched it. I was too ashamed to look at Charmaine. I touched the match to the pile and watched as Cindy's lace panties and padded bras disappeared inside the flames. I thought about Johnny, how much we had in common now, and what it would be like to go home tomorrow and watch my father lie.

I wanted to be back in my bed at home, before the fire, before everything got so complicated. I looked at Charmaine and tapped her on the shoulder. "Tag. You're it."

I ran through the woods as fast as I could, hearing the comforting sound of her breath as she ran behind me.

Bottle Tree Blues

Kelly met Silas on the bar at The Cavern. "On the bar," she'd repeat when people asked if she meant 'in the bar.' She stood on the bar as she swayed from side to side. She was losing her religion—right there in front of everybody.

The band had gotten low down. The singer was wailing. Kelly moved her arms and hips in time. They were all one – people in the half-dark listening, the band, her, and old Jack the bartender, who never stopped pouring no matter what.

Then Silas jumped up on the bar beside her.

"This girl can dance," he proclaimed to the crowd. Kelly looked down and saw his big man feet on the bar. The toe of his mud-caked boot hung a full three inches over the edge.

He'd broken her spell. It didn't matter that he had green eyes, sandy brown hair, and a cleft in his chin, as if God had picked him special and run a fingernail through his chin before his face was set.

Her hips slowed, and her hands floated down to her sides. But then she saw his face. He was gone too. He moved from side to side, his arms in the air. His face looked just like the faces of folks at the Free Will Baptist Church when they got the spirit.

She leaned over and kissed him on the lips. The bar cheered. Kelly and Silas hopped off the bar.

After that, they were Cavern regulars. Silas talked sports with the old men sitting around the bar. Kelly poured their beers when Jack went out for a smoke.

Kelly loved Silas because he was what her English teacher had called "authentic." What you saw was what you got. She saw a big boy who loved music and shooting and didn't look beyond the next beer. Having no plans was fine with Kelly.

Her parents had been so full of plans that they'd left her with her grandmother Adelaide when she was five, and went off to California. She remembered her mother's red lipstick and Eau de Joy perfume.

"You be good now, baby," her mother whispered in her ear before they drove away.

When they were gone, Granny tried everything she could think of to distract Kelly. She took her colored glass bottles off the kitchen windowsill and hung them on the branches of the small cypress in back of the house.

"It's called a bottle tree," she told Kelly. "My Mama told me they would chase away the blues. See how the light shines on those bottles."

As they sat on the lawn staring up at the tree, a wind came

up. The wind blew past the mouths of the bottles making a low moaning sound.

"You hear that. Now the bottles have all your sadness," said Granny, stroking Kelly's hair.

Every Christmas Kelly got a postcard with an orange on the front. *Wish you were here* was scrawled on the back in her mother's script, along with a series of x's and o's.

Kelly knew they were never coming back. After her 13th birthday, she quit pretending that they were going to send her a plane ticket or show up at the door.

The tree in back grew, pushing the bottles toward the sun, pushing Kelly's sadness further and further away. Granny and Kelly talked and cooked and sang songs on the porch at night.

When Kelly was sixteen, her granny started forgetting things. But, Kelly saw the pure joy in Granny's face when she noticed a flower in the yard, as if for the first time. Kelly decided that it was okay to live in the moment.

The next year, Granny went to the nursing home. A year later, she died, leaving Kelly the house and the pair of striped pajamas she'd worn with "Addie" written on the label with a laundry marker. Kelly wore them to sleep in. Memories were all she had left of her family. Silas never spoke of his family.

He took her riding in his truck through the mountains. He'd drive down the hills really fast. She'd laugh when her stomach dropped just like on the roller coaster, and he'd smile. They'd go into the woods where he'd line up beer and whiskey bottles he kept in the back of the truck. Even after a six-pack, he could take them out without missing a single one.

"You're my sweet girl," he'd whisper, when they lay down in the grass. She'd rub her thumb across his callused palm as if there was a secret hidden there that she could feel out, like the blind reading Braille.

Kelly showed Silas the bottle tree, but he just laughed and muttered something about an "old wives tale."

Silas had come to Laurel from Jackson. Tired of big city life, he said. But Kelly had found a summons folded up into a small square in the corner of his wallet when she was looking for money to pay the pizza delivery man. Reckless driving, assault, public drunkenness. What's one bad night? she thought. He was usually a happy drunk, singing and dancing, like that first night on the bar.

They slept together, played together, drank together, and lived together. It was four months after they met that Kelly went off beer. Its smell made her queasy. No matter how much she wanted a drink, it would come back up on her. A month later, her jeans wouldn't fit, and she figured she was pregnant.

"I'm going to be a daddy?" asked Silas, standing a little taller. He celebrated by downing a fifth of whiskey and singing "Rock a Bye, Baby" in the general direction her stomach. *My baby's daddy*, she thought to herself.

Later that night, Kelly sat in the rocker and knitted a blanket for the baby in alternating pink and blue, while Silas snored loudly from the couch.

After a while, she stopped going to The Cavern. The smoke got to her, and watching Silas get drunk was different when she was sober. He'd talk slow, like his brain was plugged up. His sleep was restless.

Kelly painted the largest closet a pale yellow and found a used bassinet at a yard sale. It barely fit inside. She cleared a patch of land in the back yard and planted carrots and peas. When the green shoots appeared, she imagined herself in the kitchen making baby food.

She was just seven months when she felt her first contraction, a rolling tightness in her belly. She got in the truck and drove to The Cavern.

Kelly could hear the blues from outside. She stopped for a minute, remembering the night she met Silas, the pulsing rhythm of the music, the sting of the beer as it slid down her throat, his mouth hard on hers.

She pushed open the door and stopped short of the threshold. Silas stood on the bar, his feet hanging over the edge. She felt like she was outside herself and half-expected to see herself dancing on the bar. But the girl next to Silas wasn't her. She was a skinny blond in tight jeans with her hand around Silas's arm as she tried to stay upright on the bar.

Kelly stood in the doorway, heavy as a boulder, while her stomach convulsed with a contraction. Silas jumped off the bar as she turned to go. "Wait a minute, Kelly. It's nothing," he yelled after her.

"Stupid bastard," she screamed. She lowered the bed of

the truck. Crying, she reached around into the back of the truck, grabbed a bottle, and threw it at Silas. He ducked. The bottle hit the grass and rolled a few feet. She kept throwing until the bed of the truck was empty.

Silas stood with his arms across his face. Kelly crouched in pain. Jack came out of the bar, took the keys, and led Kelly into the truck.

Addie was born three hours later. She had Kelly's blue eyes and Silas' cleft chin. Kelly ran her thumb across it. *All I have left of him*, she thought and held the baby close.

She slept fitfully and looked forward to the times when Addie came to nurse. She began to imagine life without Silas' sloppy joy.

When she brought Addie home four days later, Kelly could hardly believe her eyes. The cypress out front was stripped of its leaves, and a bottle hung from the end of each branch. Budweiser, Jim Beam, Jack Daniels, Pabst Blue Ribbon bottles hung in the air, catching the sunlight.

Kelly stood there, her baby in her arms, the silence broken only by the moan of the wind as it blew past the mouths of the bottles. She let the sound carry her sadness away.

Helter Skelter

My sister Amber told me not to stare at the sun or I'd go blind. She also told me that Beatle's song "Helter Skelter" drove some guy crazy and he formed a cult and murdered people. I didn't listen to the radio for a while after that. I still look at the sun though. I can't help it. It's up there, daring me to look. My father hardly ever sees the sun. He works nights at the Ford plant and sleeps during the day. Sometimes early in the morning I feel him kiss my forehead.

Once I woke up to find him kneeling by the bed just looking at me and Amber. She slept beside me, on her side of the bed, which was two inches bigger than my side. She put blue painter's tape down the middle of the bed. When I crossed it, Amber pinched me. When she was out riding her bike, I measured it. I never learned to ride a bike, though Dad swears he taught me. I'm not the athletic type, which is good because if I was, I wouldn't have anyone to play ball with anyway.

I hang out with Lucy from down the street. She has glasses and feathered hair. We walk down to the library and buy candy at the convenience store. Amber rides her bike and sometimes rides in cars with boys. She made me swear not to tell dad. Every now and then, she'd throw me a bag of candy and say "for our little secret." I don't believe in secrets. Sooner or later, everything comes out. Like the truth about our Mama. Dad said she was killed in an accident. But I saw in the newspaper that her car broke down on the highway and that she stepped out into traffic. Right into it. I wonder if the sun got in her eyes and she just couldn't see where she was going. Those things happen.

Strange things happen all the time. Like when I saw a girl who looked just like Amber smoking in front of Mike's Pub. Mike's is where the old guys sit and drink beer in the afternoon. I pass by there sometimes and glance in. It's dark inside, with clouds of cigarette smoke. The television over the bar always has a game on. Old guys are hunched over on stools.

Dad quit going to Mike's after mom died. All he does now is work and sleep. He wakes up in time for dinner, which Amber made from a box. Spaghetti from a box. Chicken casserole from a box. Macaroni and cheese from a box. When she was in a real bad mood, she'd "forgot" to drain the grease off the hamburger before adding it to the noodles. I ate dinner Lucy's on the days Amber made meatloaf. Her meatloaf was nasty. Now we have takeout.

Mama was a good cook. She'd feed me bits of carrot or jelly beans from a jar as she cooked. She'd dance around the kitchen while the food cooked. She always drained the grease.

She hung wind chimes over the kitchen sink even though there is no wind in the kitchen. She'd run her fingers across the chimes to hear the notes. It was my favorite sound. Now, my favorite sound is the theme song to the Flintstone's, where you get to meet them and know all about them. I'm pretty sure Amber's favorite sound was a Beatle's song, even though they drove that man crazy. Crazy like Jim, who came back from Vietnam with a tattoo of a heart on his palm. He goes up to people on the street and screams, "Look at the sacred, bleeding heart of Jesus." I looked, but I didn't see any blood.

Sometimes there were spots of blood on our bed sheets when I didn't cut myself. I showed Amber and she said told me to shut up. She was so touchy. She hated for me to touch her stuff. I'd play her records and put on her white blouse with the gold threads running through it and look through her drawers. In her underwear drawer, I found the map to her secret place in the office park across from the Ford Plant. The office park is full of plain white buildings, but in the middle of the parking lot there is a waterfall. If you walk past it and follow the path up the hill, there is small circle of fir trees. Inside the tree, there is a place with logs to sit on. I went there once during the daytime – the ground was covered with beer bottles, and something that looked like the finger of a glove was lying in the dirt. The place looked kind of nasty if you ask me, which no one ever does.

I woke up in the middle of the night one night, and Amber was gone. I was pretty sure she went to her secret place. I thought about moving the blue painter's tape or spending the rest of the night trying on everything in her closet, but I decided to go and find her instead. I got dressed and put my house key around my neck. I got out my bike and headed for the secret place. Man, was it quiet at night. I passed dark houses and thought of Lucy snuggled under her comforter in her quiet, pink bedroom. I thought of Dad working the line at Ford, the air humming with noise. Then I thought about Amber hidden in the pine trees and wondered what it would feel like to do anything you wanted.

As I got to the office park, a pink light was spreading the sky. I leaned my bike against a boulder and started up the path. I could hear sounds above me. Breathing, trees shaking, grunts and gasps of air. I ran the rest of the way and into the space between the trees. Some guy had Amber against the tree. Her jeans and panties were around her ankles. Her eyes got really wide when she saw me.

"I'll go get help," I yelled and started running down the path.

"Jake, get off me," Amber yelled. Then "Sarah, come back."

I ran through the office park and toward the road that separated the park from the Ford Plant. Shift change. Cars were leaving the plant parking lot, their drivers eager for a cup of coffee, a drink, or a warm bed. I timed it just right and made it through the traffic and across the street. I looked back to see Amber running after me. She wore her Rolling Stones t-shirt, the one with the tongue on it. She didn't see the car. She was looking at the horizon and the pink morning sun on a bed of clouds.

I love the Rolling Stones, who as far as I know have never driven anyone crazy. I like their song about clouds. I imagine Amber on her cloud, other angels come to visit. I bet when she gets tired of them she says, "Hey you get offa my cloud." I hate their song "Paint it Black." It reminds me of the darkness and all the things I've ever lost. Stuff that rolled under my bed or just disappeared. When it comes on the radio, I go out in the front yard and look up to the sky. I find the sun and take a good long look until everything goes red and I have to close my eyes.

Neverland

The brown circle around her eye might have been a shadow. Yellow-tinged fingerprint marks around her wrist peeked out from under her sleeve. I looked away, went on coloring. I handed her raw sienna, burnt umber, and Indian red. I stared at my coloring book, working hard to stay within the lines.

***

The bruises were the first thing I thought of when I saw Eileen in the grocery. She looked tired. She had grown her hair out from the wedge cut that was so popular when we were kids. Her hair was long now; it framed her face. It was a brassier blond. She wore little half glasses on her nose. Still, I could see shadows of the girl I'd known.

Eileen rolled the cart slowly, scanning the rows of cereal. She picked out a huge box of sugar-frosted flakes. My eyes moved reflexively to the canister of oatmeal in my cart.

I turned toward the granola as we passed each other, half hoping she would pass me by, and felt her hand on my arm.

"Angie?"

I looked at her, feigning surprise. "Eileen? I can't believe you recognized me after all this time."

"You look the same."

"You too," I said, waiting for my giveaway. I felt my lip curl into a half smile as I lied.

"What are you up to these days?" she asked.

"I have a small catering business," I said.

"I'm not surprised. Remember we used to help your mom make cookies every Saturday?" she said.

I caught myself looking at her wrists. She wore a red sweater, and its cuffs were folded back neatly. Her skin was free of marks.

I'd lived in the Margate Apartments when I knew Eileen. The populace was a strange mix of the newly divorced, corporate transients, and young professionals. Mine was the only intact family there. I didn't know it then, but that would change in the next year. My parents' arguments would become more frequent, and my father would move into his own small unit in an apartment complex a mile away.

It was a painful time for me, one I always associated with the apartments and the children who had lived there. So much sadness lurked in those hallways: breakups, lost jobs, divorce, abuse. Of course, I didn't know that then. But, there was a menacing impermanence manifested by the U-Haul trucks that came and went from the complex.

"How about you? I asked.

"Okay. I work part time in an accounting firm. I was in

California for a while, but I came home when Mom got sick. She passed last year."

I remembered hearing Eileen's mother shout as I came up the hall to their apartment. My hands would tingle the closer I got. Eileen came to the door, her face pink, but smiling, always smiling. "Let's play at your house today," she would say. So, we did.

"Oh, Eileen. I'm sorry for your loss." I reached out to hug her. I could feel her arms stiffen as I reached around her shoulders.

I was surprised. We had shared a bed during sleepovers and pressed our fingers together, merging globes of blood from a pinprick. I'd grabbed her arms when I tagged her during manhunt. Sometimes we'd hide together, so close I could feel the hair on her arms touch mine.

All the kids in the complex played manhunt. It was hide and seek, but no one wanted to call it by its baby name. We waited until dusk, designated someone as "it," and ran in all directions looking for a place to hide. We lingered in hallways and hid in utility closets. We hid behind bushes and next to dumpsters. It took hours for us to find each other.

"She went quickly, didn't suffer," Eileen said, stepping back.

Not like you? Were you tempted to hit her back? Were you glad to see her go? I asked these questions in my head, as we stood awkwardly blocking the aisle.

"I should let you go," Eileen said, her hands perched on the handle of her cart.

As she pushed her cart past mine, I reached out to touch

her back. She didn't turn around. "You remember those summer nights at dusk? Manhunt? We were so young," I said.

"Free," she said, turning back to me. "We were so free during those hours."

I nodded.

She hesitated. "I'm having a small work party at my house and could use someone to help with the food. Can I call you?"

I handed her my card. I noticed that she kept her nails trimmed short, unpolished.

***

I brought the standard fare of assorted sandwiches and chocolate-dipped fruit with a cheesecake for dessert. Eileen's house was a small, trim bungalow in a neighborhood popular for its unique shops and central location. She gave me a key so I could set up that afternoon. I carried a cooler into the kitchen and began putting the food in the fridge. Eileen had left space for the food. I scanned the shelves—leftover lasagna, egg salad, a single lemon. She had three mid-range bottles of pinot grigio chilling. Four bottles of red wine lined the countertop. Tucked behind the condiments on the lower shelf was a tooth whitening kit. I wasn't sure why it needed refrigeration, but was intrigued all the same.

"Eileen," I said loudly.

There was no answer. I hesitated before heading upstairs. I had always been nosy. I once tried to sneak a peek at my mother's checkbook only to find a large spider inside.

As children, Eileen and I had once shared a toothbrush. We had called each other each night to say goodnight. She comforted me when my parents fought. Then Mom and I moved to an apartment across town. I made new friends. Eileen and I quit calling each other. Time had erased our intimacy. Still, I felt we had unfinished business.

The stairs squeaked as I climbed. I came to a hallway with three doors, two bedrooms and a bathroom. The walls were the same blank white as the apartment. The bathroom had a flowered shower curtain. The tub was spotless. A single bottle of shampoo sat on the ledge of the tub.

The medicine cabinet held hair ties and toothpaste tubes. There was a row of pill bottles on the bottom shelf – thyroid medicine, acid reducer, and something called Vilox.

The smaller bedroom could have been a display room in a department store. A floral comforter covered the bed. Matching floral prints hung on the walls. A pedestal in the corner with a matching vase held silk flowers. The closet held old coats and sweaters. The small bookshelf was full of paperbacks, beach books: stories of romance, crime, and friendship.

The master bedroom was large. A white comforter covered a queen bed. I recognized the headboard from childhood. It had been her mother's and was made of cherry wood carved with vines and had two hummingbirds meeting in the middle, their beaks touching. The few times we were in the apartment alone, I remembered running my fingers across the birds, willing them to come to life. I'd imagine Eileen's stern mother chasing the birds around the room. As girls, we had laughed at that, though Eileen's laugh was guarded, as if her mother might hear her, even though she was at the grocery six blocks away.

I touched the figures of the birds, wondering if Eileen's mother had kissed her when she tucked her in at night. Did she ever feel guilty?

Eileen's dresser was new. The top of it was scattered with earrings, rings, and a necklace. A greeting card reading Fifty Fabulous Years of You sat open. It was signed by someone named Karen. A small picture of Eileen at her college graduation was in the center of the dresser, her cap slightly askew, her smile close-lipped, as if she had something to say, but was too polite to say it.

I kept looking, unsure of what I was looking for until I found it. In the bottom drawer of the dresser, under an old sweater, there was a stack of pictures. Eileen as a baby, swaddled and perched in her mother's arms. Her mother smiled at Eileen's father, a stern young man who looked into the camera, with a piercing glare. He was long gone by the time I met Eileen. She never spoke of him.

There was five-year-old Eileen on the couch with a huge book propped on her lap. She studied the pages as she held on to the sides of the book.

The next picture startled me. In it, Eileen and I stood on the edge of the swimming pool, long limbed and unself-conscious. She with her grownup wedge cut, a silly grin on her face. I with braids, my head turned to look at her, smiling tentatively.

I had a mother who loved me. I would go on to graduate from college, marry, have two daughters, and divorce. Pictures of my loved ones hung on walls and adorned the mantle. Most of Eileen's were in a drawer.

I searched our faces, not sure what I hoped to find. I sat on the edge of her bed, washed in sadness. I mourned the girl in the picture who took the blows and went on acting as if everything was normal. I mourned for myself, for my confusion and complicity, for the way I clung to innocence in the face of the hard reality, not letting myself acknowledge what was happening to Eileen or the impending breakdown of my own family.

I tucked the pictures back in place and went downstairs to dress the table. I had just finished setting out the sandwiches when Eileen came in from work.

She poured me a glass of wine, and we stood by the glass doors that overlooked her patio. The sky was starting to darken.

"It's not too late, you know," she said, casting me a sidelong glance.

"For what?"

"We can ditch all this and go play manhunt."

I imagined Eileen hiding near the dumpster in her skirt and high heels. We smiled at each other.

It was too late, but I wouldn't be the one to say so.

I knew then we would never talk about the old days, not in a way that mattered. It would stay a Neverland, equal parts innocence and menace, which we survived only to find each other on the other side.

Like I Miss Not Being a Ballerina

I don't mind being home alone after school. My father is always painting cars in his garage shop, and my brothers, Anders and Theo, are off on their bikes. There's always television. I can name the afternoon lineup on all the channels. There are game shows where people say "boobies" and comedies that feature pretty women who are witches and genies.

When I watch the sitcoms, I wonder why those women don't leave. The men in those shows tell them not to use their powers, and they do, and something goes wrong, and they always have to fix it, but they never get any of the credit. Why aren't they flying to Paris or conjuring up great mounds of candy instead of listening to their husbands?

I spend my allowance on candy. My best friend Sheila Campbell and I meet on the corner on Saturday mornings and walk up to the convenience store together. The store has a great collection – smarties, tootsie rolls, kits taffy, wax lips, and sugar babies. We walk out with brown paper sacks weighed down with goodies.

Sometimes we sit on the curb and eat most of the candy right then. Sheila's mother notices when she doesn't eat dinner, but my dad just heats up soup or slaps some cold cuts on a plate so we can all make our own sandwiches. He doesn't watch to make sure we eat, although sometimes at night he asks if I had enough to eat, and the look of love on his face makes my heart ache.

Sheila calls me at night, and we watch Sonny and Cher on television while we talk. My brothers sit on the couch behind me, nudging each other whenever Cher shows up in a low cut top.

"Look at that!" Sheila whistles.

"Would your mom let you wear a tube top like that?" I ask.

"Never, ever, ever," she says.

"My dad would have a fit," I say, mostly to fit in. I'm not sure he would notice if I wore a tube top.

"Don't worry," says Theo. "You'll never look like Cher."

I pretend not to hear him.

When I turned eleven, Dad asked Mrs. Hester next door to take me to the department store. She took me to the chubby section. I didn't let her into the dressing room. I took a moment to examine my tummy in the mirror. It stuck out a little. I patted it gently. I liked it, a soft place to rest my arms at night.

Mrs. Hester insisted on getting me a pair of jeans known for their durability, not style. I imagined them lasting me well into my twenties. When I got home, I hid them in the back of my closet.

As the show was ending, Sonny and Cher brought their daughter Chastity out. I knew enough to know that her name was ironic.

"Aww," I say.

"That Chastity is so cute. Charlotte, when I have a girl I'm gonna call her Chastity or Scarlet," says Sheila.

I don't plan to have any kids. I'm going to travel, maybe be a reporter like the ones on the news. I might get to meet Walter Cronkite.

"I'm gonna call my daughter Brooke or Kristie," I say.

After the show, I go to my room to read until Dad comes to tuck me in. He's good at tucking me in. He pulls the covers up to my chin and kisses my forehead.

"Say it, Dad."

"Everybody to their own thing, said the old lady as she bent down to kiss the cow's behind."

I laugh into my pillow.

"Goodnight, Char," he says, as he closes my door.

I'm usually fine with the no mother thing, except on Mother's Day, when everybody is rubbing your face in it. Of course, I have a mother. She died when I was four from a heart abnormality. My father says she was one of a kind, a real original. I don't imagine her in heaven. I imagine her on the beach in Florida, sunning herself in a svelte black swimsuit, a handsome pool boy bringing her drinks and snacks as her body warms in the sun. In my version, she's on vacation from her job as a top ranking engineer at NASA.

I miss her, but in a strange way, like I miss not being a ballerina. I'd love to dance, but I'm clumsy, so I eliminated ballerina from my career aspirations long ago, though tutus are so cool, and I would love to wear the shoes that tie up with pink ribbons.

I can't remember my mom at all. All I have to go on are old photographs. In one picture, she looks down at me with a look of wonder that could only be caused by a double rainbow. I look at it when I'm alone and say, "That's love" out loud, over and over.

School is okay. I like most of my classes. I have one problem with sixth grade—mandatory physical education class. I hate the outfit, a polyester one-piece in blue and white stripes that makes me look fat and shows off my dimpled knees. Sheila says we look like escapees from a women's prison.

Tuesday is dodge ball day. Ms. Foster makes us count off so I end up on a different team from Sheila. I stand in the center of the circle with the kids on my team. Bobby Siefert holds the ball and eyes the bunch of us.

"Watch out, wide load," he says, heaving the ball at me. I sidestep to my left. The ball whizzes past and hits Kathy Cantrell. Kathy is skinny and pale. There's an angry red mark where the ball hit her leg.

Sheila catches the rebound and throws the ball as far away from me as she can. I can only hide out for so long. Bobby gets the ball again.

"Do I get extra points for bagging big game?" he asks. Several boys laugh. The ball hits me hard in the stomach. As I make an "ouff" sound and double over, the ball bounces off me and hits Sam Anderson and Alice Teel. I stand up and try to pretend like it didn't hurt.

"Thanks, Charlotte," says David Pascal. My team grumbles.

When we are getting dressed, Sheila tells me not to listen to those dummies.

There's a red mark on my tummy that lasts until bedtime.

The next day, Sheila is absent from school. I call her that night so we can talk about *Welcome Back Kotter*, but her father answers the phone and says Sheila will call me back tomorrow.

Sheila shows up at my door in the morning with two packets of Pop-Tarts. She hands me one, and we sit on the front stairs to eat. Her lips quiver.

"My mom is sick." She bursts into tears. I take our Pop-Tarts and place them wrapper side down on the steps to avoid germs. I put my arm around Sheila and feel her body heave with sobs. "Cancer," she whispers.

I pat her back and say, "there, there," which is something I got from Alice the maid on *The Brady Bunch* who always seems to be comforting someone. When Sheila calms down, we finish our Pop-Tarts and walk to school.

"You don't even look like you've been crying." I don't lie very often, which makes me convincing when I do.

In pictures, my mom has jet-black hair that comes to a widow's peak at her forehead. She always smiled and looked straight into the camera. I can't remember her voice or her touch. Mrs. Campbell has flyaway brown hair cut into a bob. She likes to sing under her breath, and her hands are always warm. She kisses me good night like I am her daughter. She hugs us before bed, and just when I think she's letting go, she pulls me in again.

Thursday afternoon, Mrs. Campbell goes into surgery. Sheila begs her father to let me come to the hospital, but he says the rule is family only. That afternoon, I'm nervous so I turn on the television. The beautiful witch on the sitcom accidentally turns her neighbor into a frog. I watch as she rushes around frantically trying to reverse the spell.

I know that in real life there is no reversing anything; everything goes forward. That's the thing about television; it offers all these wild dreams.

The phone rings. I know it's Sheila. I know what I would wish for if I had special powers. I take a deep breath and answer the phone.

Skipping Stones

The beer, her first, tasted bitter to Terri, but she didn't stop drinking until the can was empty. It was her first real high school party. Terri wore her new blue sleeveless shift that she bought with her mother at Stewart's in Louisville. It was the color of dusk. It was a dress to be noticed in.

Greg Thompson's parents had gone to Glasgow to see a community theater production of *Bye Bye Birdie*, leaving their sons unsupervised for the night. Greg was well-liked because he was funny and would do anything on a dare. Greg's older brother bought a few cases of Falls City beer. The cans went into a trash bag on the patio.

Shayne Phillips was on the patio crushing cans with his feet. Small groups gathered around, perched on patio furniture, standing on the lawn. Terri felt dizzy as she watched Shayne's mud-caked boot turn a can into a flat aluminum disc. Shayne tossed the can into the garbage bag and reached out to steady her.

"The first time I drank, I felt lousy, all woozy and separate from everything," said Shayne.

"How do I make it stop?" Her bare shoulder brushed his flannel shirt.

"Eat something, and you'll feel better."

She'd never been this close to Shayne. He was tall and had a smattering of freckles that covered his face. Shayne was quiet and spent his afternoons working in his family's grocery store. She'd known him forever but had never really seen him.

Terri felt herself being lifted and spun in slow circles. She reached her arms out towards Shayne. She smelled Greg's cologne and felt his arms tight around her waist.

"Stop it!"

She heard Greg's laugh, felt his breath on her neck.

"Let go of me!" said Terri.

She thought she might be sick and knew that if she did, it would be the only thing people would remember her for, not her shiny dark hair or that she worked on the school paper or was an aide at the library. She'd be known forever after as the girl who vomited at Greg Thompson's party.

"Put her down!" said Shayne. He grabbed Greg's arm.

Greg set Terri down and rounded on Shayne with a left hook. His class ring clipped Shayne in the mouth, and blood poured from Shayne's lip.

"Hit him back," said Pete Phillips, Shayne's older brother.

"They're fighting over you," said Pam. Seeing Pam's face flushed with excitement made Terri sick to her stomach again.

"Gross, Pam." She walked towards the boys. "Stop—right now!" She impersonated her mother. Greg and Shayne kept swinging. "Stop!"

The boys stepped apart.

Terri saw the look of disgust on Greg's face as she pulled Shayne inside the house to bandage his lip. When they came out of the house, Greg was nowhere in sight, and Pam was deep in conversation with Silas Hunt.

"You want some crackers or something?" asked Shayne.

"No," said Terri. "I just want to go home."

"Can I walk you?"

"No, thanks."

Terri walked down the quiet streets enjoying the cool air on her face. Though the excitement of the fight had sobered her up, she was still woozy. Terri stumbled as she crossed the Andersons' lawn and fell. Green marred the perfect blue of her dress. A grass stain. God knows what her mother would think happened. She planned to hide the dress under her bed. Later, she would sneak it into the washing machine.

As she walked past windows lit up by television, Terri thought about the future. This was her last year of high school, and Terri felt as if she were finally figuring out what she was interested in. She had begun eating her lunch in the library, sitting at a small round table with the librarian Miss Allen, who was tall and beautiful.

Terri loved the hopeful silence of the school library. The bowed heads of the students as they leaned over books reminded her of church without the heavy feeling in the air.

She wondered what it would be like if Miss Allen was her

mother—someone poised and well read. She couldn't imagine Miss Allen sobbing for hours or throwing a fit. Whenever things were crazy at home, Terri visualized Miss Allen sitting at the library table sipping tea from a delicate china cup. Though she'd never seen her with a man, Terri bet lots of men fought over Miss Allen.

The librarian had introduced Terri to Jane Austen. Getting lost in Austen's long sentences and antique cadences, one beautiful phrase after another, reminded Terri of wandering through a field of wildflowers.

Terri imagined herself in the future, wandering the stacks of a large public library, putting each book in its place, then taking the subway to a small apartment that was all her own. Not in a frilly pink room in a house where her mother watched her every move, as if Terri's life was a movie presented for her approval or, more often, disapproval.

When she got home, her mother was asleep on the couch clutching a pillow to her chest. Her mother slept a lot. Terri tiptoed into her bedroom. She peeked into her parents' room. Her father wasn't home. He was rarely home, and when he was, his mind was elsewhere. He asked Terri about school but never listened to her answer.

School was strange on Monday. Terri could feel the stares as she walked down the hall. As she passed, girls talked behind their hands about the fight. Guys who never noticed her were staring at her. When she saw Greg in the lunchroom, he acted like she was invisible.

She was relieved to escape to the library in fifth period. She was working the desk when Shayne came in carrying *Heart of Darkness*.

"How was it?"

"Dark," said Shayne.

"Funny," said Terri.

As he walked away, she noticed a piece of paper sticking out between the pages.

On it, he scrawled, *Gordon's Pass 3:30.*

Terri had been to Gordon's Pass once. When she was little, she and her father had gone there to give her mother "some peace and quiet." Her father brought a fishing rod. She remembered sitting next to him on a large boulder, his hands over hers as he guided the fishing rod, while mist from the water dotted her arms.

***

Terri propped her bike against a tree. The road ahead of her curved out of sight around a bend. She stood on the side of the stream and then jumped from rock to rock until she was on a small rock in the center of the water. She looked up at the sunlight on the mountain face, at the brush that clung to the mountainside. She looked down at the water streaming by, bouncing off the rocks. A rock skipped in the water in front of her. She turned; Shayne was standing on the bank.

Terri retraced her path across the boulders as Shayne sent another rock skipping across the water.

"Show me how to do that."

"Look for flat rocks," he said. Shayne showed her how to bend her arm parallel to the ground as she held the stone between her thumb and forefinger.

"Swing your arm forward and let go."

Terri threw the rock. It skipped across the water twice.

Shayne threw his rock. "One, two, three, four, five six."

"You're a jerk. You know that, don't you?" Terri smiled.

He reached into his pocket and handed her a perfectly flat rock. She threw it.

It skipped four times. They sat down on a boulder by the side of the stream. Shayne picked at the grass nearby.

"I'm sorry," he said, not meeting her eyes. "About the fight. I just wanted him to leave you alone."

"Thanks, but no more fighting."

"Do you want me to leave now?"

"No," said Terri.

If he kisses me, I'll kiss him back, thought Terri, but he didn't try.

They sat in silence, listening to the wind blow through the grass, watching the colors of the sun refracted in the mist.

***

Terri could smell hamburgers and baked beans when she entered the house. The vacuum was in the middle of the room, and stacks of folded laundry lined the couch. Her mother sat at the dining room table, a plate full of uneaten food in front of her, smoking a Pall Mall. "You're late. Where've you been?"

"Gordon's Pass."

"Who were you with?"

"Shayne Phillips."

"You shouldn't be hanging around boys by yourself."

"We weren't doing anything."

"You had to be doing something."

"Skipping stones."

Terri's mother looked her in the eye. "Nobody likes a prick tease, dear," she said, plunging her cigarette into the baked beans.

***

Terri was walking home from school, having taken sick in the middle of the day. Her hand rested on her achy throat. As she walked down Main Street, she saw her father driving out of town. He didn't see her. When she got home, her mother was on the couch crying. The coffee table was piled with cards, letters, and pictures.

"This is all I have of him anymore. Bits of paper! Throw it out. Throw it all out."

Terri placed a layer of waxed paper on top of the trash before filling it with her father's mementos. She had a feeling her mother would be pulling them out before long. But that night in bed, she heard the ring of the garbage can lid as her mother slammed it down.

Her father moved to South Point with his secretary. Terri got a part time job at The Good Enough Diner to get away from the house and her mother's tears. She loved the flow of taking orders, pouring refills, waiting for the cook to ring the bell telling her an order was up.

Occasionally, she would notice a look of pity on a customer's face or find a large tip on the table. Just last week, Abby Linder left three dollars, and this was after having to remind Terri to refill her coffee twice.

On Wednesday nights, Miss Allen sat in the booth in the corner and ordered her regular, tuna salad on white bread with lettuce and catsup, black coffee, and apple pie.

She'd leave two dollars and a new book on the table. This week it was *Anna Karenina*.

Shayne would come in too and order coffee black, which he would blow on until it cooled, watching the diners over his cup. Occasionally he would take a sip.

"You don't really drink coffee, do you?" asked Terri.

Shayne pretended to look offended and raised his mug for a small sip.

"Want some sugar?" asked Terri.

"No"

"Milk or cream?"

"No, thank you."

He'd leave her fifty cents.

Sometimes his brother Pete came along too. He'd sit at the counter jiggling his leg. He'd blow his straw paper across the room and eat all the meringue off of his pie, leaving the banana custard. He was a lousy tipper.

When she got home, Terri's mother would either be in a deep sleep or wide awake and ready to remind Terri of all the ways she was like her father. Terri took a second job shelving books at night at the town library. If she got home at eleven, there was a better chance her mother would be fast asleep.

Two nights a week, she went straight from the diner to the library. She took the golden skeleton key from the bottom of her purse and felt the bolts release as she turned the key. The heavy door opened slowly. Terri locked the door behind her.

She stood for a moment drinking in the silence before she turned on the bank of lights that shown directly over the stacks. She found the trolley stacked with books next to the front desk. They were arranged by Dewey Decimal number, waiting to be returned to their correct spot. She was comforted by the thought that there was a correct place for every book.

Because she could see the withdraw cards, Terri was privy to the secret lives of her taciturn neighbors. She discovered that Wally the barber read biographies of great composers, Abby Linder dipped into *Grimm's Fairy Tales,* and Linda Starnes was interested in the drawings of Leonardo da Vinci. She moved among the aisles completely at ease until the trolley was empty and it was time to go home.

***

Terri volunteered to work the food table at prom so she wouldn't have to worry about being asked to the dance. In between refilling the plates, she searched the room for Shayne. When she was emptying chips into a large bowl, Greg Thompson asked her to dance.

"It's the least you can do really, after ruining my party and all," he said.

She said no, but Greg stopped by the table after each dance.

"If I dance with you, will you leave me alone?" asked Terri. She wasn't sure he even liked her. He was used to getting his way.

It was a slow dance, and Greg pulled Terri against the front of his tuxedo. She tried to step back, but he held her close.

"Greg! I can't breathe."

He had his hand firmly on the small of her back. She could feel him pressing against her. She was at once both revolted and curious.

She watched the clock, hoping for the song to end. When it did, Greg released her. He smirked at her. "You're welcome," he said.

Terri walked away.

***

It was her turn to close the diner, which meant wiping down tables and booths and turning the chairs upside down on the tabletops. It was hard work, and she was glad when she finished. She turned off the lights and stepped outside, locking the door beside her.

Greg Thompson sat on a bench two storefronts down. "Can I give you a lift home?"

Terri was tired and hoped he'd use the drive home to apologize for being such a jerk at prom.

She got into his father's car. Greg drove to the town square.

"Where are you going?" she asked.

"Don't you want to catch up? Don't you want to spend a little time together?"

"No," she said. "I need to go home." She felt a rush of panic.

He'd driven to his father's office at Wilson and Meer. When he pulled in front of the building, Terri thought about running away.

She stood in the doorway. She could leave now, walk home. But she didn't go. It was like standing on the edge of the high dive, that strange mixture of fear and curiosity.

She had expected a kiss, but once inside Greg pulled her onto the leather couch. She tried to stand, and he pushed her back onto the couch. She fell onto her back, and he knelt beside her, one hand on her chest, the other moving up her leg underneath her skirt.

She strained to sit up. He held her down.

"What do you think you're doing?" she asked.

"What you want me to do."

"Stop!" She slapped his face.

"That's it. Fight me."

She could feel his hand slide under her underwear, his fingers pushing inside of her. "No!" she yelled, pushing his hand away.

He smacked her face. "You want to explain a broken nose to your mother?"

His fingers were moving back and forth inside her. She grew wet in spite of herself. Bile crawled up her throat. She was a fool to go with Greg. She turned her head away and stared at a framed picture of flowers.

Terri heard the front door open.

"Don't say a word," said Greg. He pulled his hand away.

"Hello," said Terri.

Greg stood up. Terri sat up, pulled up her panties, and smoothed down her skirt. Footsteps echoed. Pete Phillips stood in the doorway carrying a bucket and mop.

"If it isn't the cleaning crew," said Greg.

Pete took in the scene, Terri's disheveled clothes and the red mark on her face, and stared at Greg, his mouth a line, his jaw pulsing. "Are you okay, Terri?"

"I need a ride home," said Terri.

"I should kill you," Pete spat at Greg.

"Hit me, and I'll have you arrested. It's your word against mine. Who'll believe the town troublemaker?" asked Greg.

They drove home in silence. Pete looked worried. Terri stared out the window, her panties damp and cold against her skin, trying to remember how she'd felt before tonight.

For a moment, she imagined them as if from above, just a boy and a girl in a car on a Saturday night. It almost seemed normal.

When they parked in front of her house, she straightened her nametag. Pete walked her to the door. "Tell me what he did to you. I'll make it right."

Terri felt like she was made of glass, like he could see inside her heart. She shook her head no.

When she got inside, Terri listened for her mother. When she heard her mother's sleeping breath through the bedroom door, Terri slid off her underwear and buried it deep in the trash.

***

On graduation day, Terri's mother showed up, her eyes rimmed in red and her dress wrinkled. Her father sat alone in the last row and handed her an envelope with a $50 bill inside. Miss Allen gave her an antique watch with a small square face of gold.

That night there was a party on the Jessup Farm on Highway 6. Terri didn't plan to go, but Shayne said she could ride with him and Pete, and they would take her home whenever she was ready to leave.

The farm was twenty miles outside of town, past abandoned barns and silos, past small white farmhouses with fancy wood work and rockers on the porch. The Jessup Farm sat back from the road. Terri could see a bonfire burning in the side yard and kids milling around.

When they got there, Pete went straight for the beer. Terri and Shayne hung back, leaning against the car as they looked up at the sky. Strands of clouds streaked across the sky, reminding Terri of cotton candy.

"What are we gonna do next?" asked Shayne.

"I want to be a librarian," said Terri.

Shayne had been offered a basketball scholarship at University of Kentucky, and there was always his parents' grocery store as a fallback. Terri wanted to go to library school, but she was overcome with guilt at the thought of leaving her mother. Her mother's fatigue and sadness had been at the center of her world for as long as she could remember. She carried it around awkwardly like a third arm.

"You need to get out of this small town. You're too smart to stay here," said Shayne.

"You mean I know better or I'm too intelligent?"

"You know what I mean."

"And you are too talented to stay. The pros will be calling."

Shayne grinned and turned to face her, putting his feet on either side of hers. She could see his freckles as he leaned in, the curve of his mouth, his eyelashes.

Not here. Not now. Terri's throat closed up, as she remembered Greg looming above her. She pushed hard against Shayne's chest, and he lurched back. Terri ran past him toward the bonfire. The sky seemed darker now and the fire brighter. She spotted Pete tossing a stick with a flame on the end of it into the air and catching it as a crowd of guys looked on admiringly.

"I have to go home, now!"

Pete threw the stick into the fire and tilted his head back, draining his bottle of beer. He threw the bottle into the grass and followed Terri to the car.

Shayne was at the wheel revving the engine, his cheeks flushed. Terri took the seat beside him, and Pete got in the back seat. Shayne floored the car, leaving tire tracks on the grass and took off down Highway 6. Terri watched the needle of the speedometer rise—50, 55, 60, 65, 70.

"Shayne. It wasn't you. I just couldn't..."

"Save it. You never liked me."

"I did. I do. I think I do. Don't do this."

The farms and barns and silos flew past in a blur as the car sped on.

"Take it to 85, brother."

"Shut up, Pete," said Terri.

"Don't."

85

"Lead."

88

"Me."

90

"On."

Terri felt herself rise in the seat as the car hit the railroad tracks and was airborne. It was a moment outside of time, when nothing had happened and anything was possible. She saw Shayne's face in profile as he looked straight ahead and heard Pete yelling from the back seat.

They landed hard. Terri's tailbone and back slammed into her seat, leaving her breathless. The car swerved wildly. Shayne turned the wheel, trying to steer out of the spin, as the car swerved into a tree on the left side. There was a crunch as they came to a stop. Glass shattered and rained down on them.

Terri moved her fingers and toes. She looked back at Pete who had a moon-shaped cut in his arm from the glass. Shayne turned toward her, wincing in pain. His shoulder was slumped, and his arm stuck out at an odd angle. It would take months to heal, and his arm would always be slightly bent.

***

That summer Terri pretended none of it had happened. During the day, she worked at the diner, cutting perfect wedges of lemon pie for Abby Linder and filling Huck Starnes' coffee cup to the two-thirds mark the way he liked it. She ran into Shayne occasionally, his arm in a cast, his hopes of playing ball shelved forever.

His broken bones healed. The finger-shaped bruises on her thighs faded to a sick yellow-green and disappeared.

That June, Pete enlisted in the Army and went to Vietnam. Terri sent him paperback novels and candy bars through the mail. Shayne worked the cash register at the grocery and used his good arm to bag groceries.

At night, Terri rolled the cart full of books through the stacks of the library, placing each book neatly on the shelf. She left with her arms full of thick novels and slim volumes of poetry.

She returned home alone and read until she fell asleep. Some nights she would dream of being back at the party, a slim half-moon like a scar in the sky and Shayne reaching out with two good arms. Before he could touch her, she'd wake up with a start.

Heavy Metal

Laura's body felt heavy. Heavy was the word her son Jason had used when he could no longer lift his head up or hold the controller to play video games. She sat by his bed reading to him like he was eight, not 16. He'd been dead four months now. She still had trouble getting out of bed. Sometimes she stayed there until noon.

She lay there while stacks of patient charts waited in her office to be coded. 204.00 was more polite than acute lymphoid leukemia without remission. In her darkest hours, Laura thought of getting 204.00 tattooed over her heart. She spent hours drawing the numbers across her chest with her fingertip.

Laura drifted off and woke to the sound of drums pounding in the apartment below. It was 12:15. She pulled on sweatpants and Jason's flannel shirt and went down to apartment 2D. She knocked on the door. The drumming didn't stop. She kicked the door, hard. Then she reached down to rub her aching foot.

"F-ing door," she shouted. The door opened to a boy, about Jason's age, with stringy jet-black hair and a nose ring.

"What do you want lady?"

"I want you to stop that damn drumming; some of us are trying to sleep."

"Don't you have, like, a job or something?" asked the kid with a smirk.

"Shouldn't you be, like, in school are something?" replied Laura. They glared at each other. A look of recognition crossed the kid's face.

"Hey, aren't you the cancer kid's mom? Jason, right?" It had been so long since anyone had spoken Jason's name. She savored the sound of it, in spite of his attitude.

"Yeah, I'm Laura." She held out her hand stiffly.

"I'm Ike," he said, lightly slapping her palm in greeting.

"Did you know Jason?"

"He lent me a pen once to take a test."

Laura smiled to herself. She could imagine him handing the pen over, his long, gorgeous fingers holding it out like a prize. Her mother had called them "piano player fingers" when Jason was a baby. His fingers were long even then and so fine that the light shone through them.

"So, like, what did you want?" Ike asked

"What were you playing?"

"Symphony of Destruction, Magadeth, do you know it?"

"No, actually I don't."

"Wanna hear me play it?"

"Sure." She followed Ike into the apartment and down a hallway lined with pictures of him at every age. She hadn't taken down the pictures at home. She half expected them to come to life, like something out of Harry Potter.

Ike's bedroom walls were covered with posters of bands. A drum kit filled the corner of the room. Laura sat on the edge of the unmade bed.

"These sticks are new. I'm still getting used to them," said Ike.

Laura nodded.

One, two, three," Ike counted off and began drumming.

The noise was fantastic. Laura could feel her heart beating. She nodded her head in time. Ike smiled. His hands flew as he beat the drums. He closed his eyes, lost in the rhythm. The cymbals crashed. Ike raised his arms, sticks in hand, in triumph. Laura laughed for the first time in months.

The music stopped, but she could feel it echoing in her ears, filling up the empty spaces.

"You wanna try it?" asked Ike, holding out the sticks. Laura took the sticks and sat behind the drum kit.

The sticks were light in her hands. Ike gave her the thumbs up and counted, "One, two, three . . ." Laura raised her arms, waiting to feel the drum beats vibrate through her fingertips straight to her heart.

Fear of Heights

When she heard Tony died, Allison thought of his hands, the way they had danced palm to palm when they were dating. She remembered the night he put his fingers through hers. It made her think of the children's game where you formed the church and steeple with your hands.

"Marry me," he whispered.

To her surprise, she said yes.

That was years ago. She had since come to believe that love was a beautiful and spiky thing.

Allison went into the backyard where Lydia bent over a patch of poppies, pulling up weeds. "We're going to Slocum."

Lydia sat up on her heels and raised her eyebrows.

"Tony died."

Lydia got to her feet and went over to put her arms around Allison. They stood in the garden together, the oversweet smell of hyacinth in the air.

***

Lydia and Allison lived just outside of Cincinnati, which

seemed like New York City after Slocum. There were German delicatessens, Unitarian churches, and art house cinemas that showed foreign movies.

The drive to Slocum was just over two hours. The highway between Cincinnati and Slocum was all fields and horse farms, except Florence with its brightly colored tower with *Florence Y'all* painted on the side. Lydia drove while Allison looked out the window.

Lydia relished the time away from the endless parade of students with their issues and questions. She was near retirement and would be relieved not to break up arguments between kids or hear their cruel taunts. She worried that the next school counselor might not know how to handle the girls whose mothers didn't prepare them for their menses. She had a cabinet stocked with pamphlets, pads, tampons, and a chart she showed the girls to explain their cycle. She told them that they could experience headaches or bloating and that they were liable to feel sad or irritable. She never called it a blessing or a curse. It was what it was.

***

Allison let her mind wander. She rarely thought of Slocum. But sometimes, in her classroom after school, when the sunlight hit the cabinets just right, she recalled Tony's hand on the small of her back and remembered how safe he made her feel. With Lydia everything was mirrored, the pitch of their voices, the curve of their bodies, the softness of their skin.

Her betrayal of Tony years ago was like a cold front that came up unexpectedly, chilling the air between her and

Lydia—and leaving Allison numb. She hated distance between them. When they reached the outskirts of Slocum, Allison reached over to hold Lydia's free hand. Lydia ran her thumb slowly across Allison's palm.

***

The first time Lydia saw Allison, she was wheeling a film projector crookedly through the hallway.

"The wheel is turned around," Lydia said. "I can fix it." She knelt and turned the wheel so that it faced forward. She saw Allison's delicate ankles above her red pumps, the bone a tender pyramid that made her think of places far more exotic than Slocum Junior High.

She took a moment to compose herself and returned to her feet.

"I'm Allison Conti. I don't think we've met." Allison extended her hand.

Lydia noticed that Allison had small fine wrists to match her ankles and a shiny gold wedding band. Her husband was Tony Conti, a carpenter.

Lydia imagined her hands encircling Allison's wrists. As they stood in the hallway talking about the upcoming break, Allison ran her hand slowly through her hair.

***

Allison had wanted a best girlfriend, someone to talk to, cook with, and share secrets with. Most of her old high school friends were immersed in having children. Their conversational repertoire ranged from infant sleep habits to the merits of breast-feeding. Babies didn't interest her. She liked kids around the age of ten, when they started having opinions about things. She liked how earnest and hopeful they were, how unafraid to share their thoughts.

Allison couldn't imagine being a mother. She still felt like a kid herself, newly married, first real job. She loved substitute teaching—geometry problems one day, the life cycle of a frog the next. The kids were funny. School was where she felt fully adult, fully in charge, until she met Lydia.

Lydia was the counselor. She had a private office and kept a journal with her wherever she went. She had blond hair, a strong chin, and the most melancholy eyes Allison had ever seen.

***

As their friendship grew, Lydia knew she would have to move slowly. She was sure Allison felt the electricity between them, and she was also positive that it confused her. She didn't want to scare Allison away. Still, she took every opportunity to touch Allison when they spent time together after school. She'd grab Allison's arm when a scene got tense at the movies.

***

Once, after school on the way to her car, Allison dropped a pile of homework papers and they blew in all directions. She and Lydia chased the papers across the parking lot laughing and screaming until they got every last one. Then Lydia threw her arms around Allison and their laughter stopped. Allison's face got serious and Lydia tugged playfully on Allison's collar.

"You have to be more careful, clumsy girl," said Lydia.

Allison felt a flutter in her stomach.

***

It was their ritual. Every Sunday evening, Tony and Allison walked hand in hand through the graveyard, which was enclosed by a brick wall. Allison's mother was buried there, and each week they brought a fresh bouquet to lay at the grave site. They walked the gravel paths, rested on the stone benches, and admired the towering oak trees. In the middle of the yard, a gazebo with a swing was ringed by tea roses. They sat down.

"How are the cabinets for Goodie's coming?"

"They're coming along. Solid oak with turned corners and long plates of glass for the kids to press their noses against."

"So Abby is happy with them?"

"Sure, why wouldn't she be?"

"She's picky, Tony." She found Tony's friend to be cold and critical.

"She's discerning," he said. "How are things at school?"

"I'm going to fill in for Sue Johansson when she goes on maternity leave."

"Her room is close to Lydia's office. You won't have to go so far to visit."

"We don't visit during school."

"I drove by just last week and saw you all eating lunch under the big oak."

"It was Lydia's birthday. I just brought a few sandwiches and cupcakes."

"I love that you have a best friend. I know you still miss your mom. It's good to have someone besides me to share things with."

"I don't need anyone else to share things with," said Allison.

"What has you so grumpy tonight?" asked Tony, pulling Allison close. For the first time ever, Allison felt like pushing him away.

***

Lydia lived in a small frame house on the edge of town. It was close enough to the railroad tracks that she could hear the train's low lonely whistle as it went through town each night at 11:30. She told Allison that she loved the quiet after a noisy day at school.

Allison was surprised by how spare the place was. A couch, low wooden coffee table, and lawyer bookshelf occupied the living room. A small glass globe with ribbons of purple inside sat on the windowsill.

A single bed with a white iron frame, a wooden dresser, and an old-fashioned rocker were the only furniture in the bedroom. "My nun's chamber," joked Lydia. A picture on the wall showed a tired looking woman in a backyard holding a baby. The yard was overgrown with weeds, and in the corner, you could see the edge of an old settee.

"We lived outside of Pikeville," said Lydia. "Three rooms,

five kids, no running water. I never would have escaped if it wasn't for the Berea College student work program."

"Were you the oldest?"

"The oldest girl, which made me chief bottle washer and babysitter. I applied for school in secret. The librarian let me use her address. I snuck out in the middle of the night, and she drove me to Berea. It was the only way I was getting out."

"Did your family come looking for you?"

"No."

"Did you ever go back?"

"No."

The tea kettle whistled.

Sit down," said Allison. Lydia watched her drop in the tea bags into the cup and pour the water on top. She wanted this moment to last forever.

***

When she felt bad for Tony, Lydia reminded herself that Allison kissed her first. They were hiking in Blenheim Forest down a trail that led to a fire tower overlooking the woods. The sun shone through the canopy, making pools of light on the forest floor. Lydia stopped Allison to show her an iridescent bug on the side of a tree. A small, green snake slithered across the path. When Allison stumbled on a rock, Lydia steadied her.

At the tower, stairs zigzagged up the interior of the steel tower to a room above. They made their way slowly up the stairs. When they reached the top, they stood in a small room with views of the forest below, Lake Devon, and the mountains in the distance.

"Breathtaking, isn't it?" asked Lydia.

"Yeah," said Allison, gasping for air.

"Are you okay?"

"Fear of heights," said Allison.

"You should have told me."

"I didn't want to spoil the fun," Allison said with a laugh.

Lydia took her hand and pulled Allison to the center of the room. "From right here you can't even tell we're up high," said Lydia, putting her arms around Allison as they faced each other. "Everything is good right here, right?"

"Yeah," said Allison.

Lydia felt Allison's heart beat fast against her own. "Let's go a bit closer," said Lydia. They moved in a slow dance until they reached the rail. Lydia turned Allison toward the rail, keeping her hands around Allison's waist. "I've got you," said Lydia. "I won't let anything happen."

While Allison looked out over the forest, Lydia buried her nose in Allison's hair. They stood in silence; the only sound was the wind blowing through the trees below.

Allison turned around and looked up at Lydia, her eyes soft. "How am I ever going to get down off of here?"

"One step at a time," said Lydia.

Allison leaned close and kissed her lightly on the lips.

When Lydia pulled her close, Allison willed her to move her hands up onto her breasts, but Lydia held her gently around the waist. Finally, they heard footfalls on the steps and parted.

That night in bed, Allison imagined herself and Lydia intertwined, pressed hard against the rail, while in the forest below, tiny fires burned away, leaving bare, dark ground.

***

Allison watched Tony sand the kitchen cabinets, his hand moving back and forth in perfect rhythm. She was sick over her betrayal. She couldn't stop replaying the moment when her lips met Lydia's, her surprise at how right it all felt. Allison had wanted that kiss and more. It reminded her of the time she pulled out into traffic at the last minute and a truck narrowly missed hitting her car. The sound of the horn made her heart beat faster, and for a moment, she felt more alive, more awake than she had ever been.

She turned to the window. Outside, the buds were coming out on the dogwood tree. Bits of green grass were sprouting on the lawn. She felt a lump rise in her throat.

She turned to Tony. He looked up at her.

"Are you all right?"

"I wouldn't hurt you for the world."

Tony looked startled. "What is it? What happened?"

"A kiss," she said, choking back sobs.

"Who is he? I'll make sure he never comes near you."

"It was Lydia. I think I love her."

Tony looked at her in disbelief. Allison reached out to touch Tony, and he stepped back, out of range.

Allison left the kitchen and went into the backyard. The yard was edged with flowerbeds, freshly tilled dirt that had been sprinkled with seeds the week before. She wouldn't be around to see them bloom.

She went back into the kitchen at dusk. Tony looked up and offered a conciliatory smile. "You'll be back," he said with certainty.

He had done this before, acted as if she didn't know her own mind, and she had surrendered to it, but not now. It would be easy to stay and succumb to the warmth and security he offered, to his goodness. She wanted more.

She packed a small bag. When she returned to the kitchen, Tony was where she had left him. She walked over and kissed him on the cheek.

Tony didn't move. He stayed there, sandpaper in hand, as he heard the front door close.

He saw her small footprint in the dust; a draft could blow it away. All it would take was one gust of the spring breeze.

***

Lydia went to see Tony at his jobsite at the Hansen place. Seth Hansen had died of old age, and his niece Adrienne was redoing the house. She hadn't told Allison she was going, knowing that it would upset her. It would be the only time she had ever been alone in a room with Tony.

Lydia knocked on the half-open front door and walked into the foyer. "Tony?"

"In here." He knelt in front of the fireplace, a stack of bricks at his side as he laid a new hearth. "Lydia, what could you possibly have to say to me?"

Lydia walked across the room and sat on the edge of the couch. "We didn't mean for it to happen. It was just one kiss, but it meant something to us both."

"You seduced her. Did you know that she'd never been kissed when I met her? She was so shy. She lost her mom when she was ten. She's confusing love with something else."

"It's not like that. Some people are just wired differently. They need something else," Lydia said gently.

"It's something else all right," said Tony.

He bent his head and continued laying the bricks and filling in the space between them with cement. Each one was perfectly placed. It was so quiet that after a while, Lydia noticed the branch of a holly tree scratching at the window. She took one last look at Tony on his knees and left.

***

Allison returned to Tony's house one afternoon to get her things. She was surprised to see his truck in the driveway. Inside, she saw that he had painted all the walls taupe, the coral living room, the yellow kitchen, and the forest green sunroom.

Through the kitchen window, she saw Tony in the backyard digging a small square patch of land. They had talked about planting a garden this year. Now it would grow without her charting its progress. She imagined plants bending over with the weight of lush tomatoes, mounds of spinach low to the ground, and flowering sage along the edges.

She climbed the stairs and found her suitcase packed and three cardboard boxes marked *Allison*. There was no trace of her anywhere in the room; the vanity was bare, and the closet held only Tony's clothes.

She heard his footsteps on the stairs. She walked further into the room and held onto the bedpost. The bed, its headboard carved with vines and roses, was his present to her when they married.

"You found your things?"

"Yes. Thank you for packing them."

"Now you can take them and go."

"I won't even have to unpack. We're moving to Cincinnati."

"In a big city like that, nobody will think twice about two bachelor girls living together."

"Sarcasm doesn't become you, Tony. You're one of the sweetest people I know."

"I'm not that man anymore. Not after this."

"I know you're hurting."

"You don't know a thing about me," he said. He picked up two of the boxes and headed down the stairs. Allison took the other box and the suitcase.

He placed the boxes carefully in the trunk of her car. She stood with her back against the car. He came to her and placed his palms against hers, his fingers through her own.

"Allison," he said, his chin resting on her head.

"Tony," she replied. His tears landed on the top of her head like an unexpected rain.

***

Tony had a plain wooden coffin, nothing polished or

carved. Allison stood by Lydia's side, holding her upper arm tightly. She wouldn't hold Lydia's hand here; everyone would talk.

"By the end, he had forgotten everything," said Abby Linder. "He was like a baby."

Allison remembered the sweet man she had loved, his kindness, the beautiful things he had created. Lydia passed her a linen handkerchief. Years as a counselor had taught Lydia when to keep her mouth shut.

After the funeral, they went to the diner and ordered pieces of banana cream pie with towering meringue. There is nothing a little sugar can't fix, Lydia's mother used to say. Lydia knew it wasn't true, then or now. She remembered the blueberry cobbler her mother would make each time she learned she was pregnant again with another child for Lydia to help raise. Lydia and her mother would sit at the kitchen table with two spoons and eat the entire pan.

***

As they rode down the highway past the white wooden fences and horse barns, Allison placed her hand in her pocket and ran her finger across the figure of a small, long-stemmed rose with one tiny thorn carved out of its side. Abby had given it to her. Tony had carved it. When Abby had come to visit Tony months before he died, he had presented it to her and said, "I made this for you, Allison."

Abby said she took Tony's hands in hers and said, "Thank you. It's lovely."

Allison put her hand in her pocket and felt the thorn sharp against her finger. She drew her hand away and placed it on her lap. She was staring out the window when she felt Lydia's hand find her own.

Emoticon

I knew Nick before we had words. Our mothers met in childbirth class. They sat next to each other in the circle. They struck up a conversation and had such a good time talking, they almost forgot the solid forms of their husbands, who sat behind them, legs spread, each supporting his wife's body with his own.

I have pictures of Nick and me as babies, snuggled into the same playpen—and shots of us riding the carousel as our mothers held us in place. The story is that he spoke first. Never an innovator, Nick's first word was "da." I spoke later. I said "ba ba," as I waved my hand goodbye.

We were best friends through grade school and then went our own ways in middle school. In high school, I was horrified to recognize my growing attraction to Nick, who had seemed more like a brother than a boyfriend. We dated all through college, sometimes barely speaking, feeling more and more like our pre-verbal selves.

Nick and I never spoke these days. We sat side by side in

coffee shops and bistros in Paris, Milan, and Geneva, and stared at our phones. Correction, he sat hunched over his phone and I watched passersby, elegant women dressed in black, teenagers in ripped jeans, working men with scruffy beards—all looking at their own small screens. Dogs peed on light poles, and birds flew like winged drones through the sky without anyone watching.

Every so often, Nick would send me a text. I knew it was him because after the ping, I could hear him let out a small sigh.

N: How r u?

He'd stare at the screen waiting for my response. I wanted to type bored, but instead I'd type F for fine. He'd go back to texting.

I watched a father and son sit side by side on a bench, both staring at their phones. After a while, the son nudged the father, but he never looked at him. The father nudged the son back, his face glued to the screen. They pushed at each other, not seeing the smile on the other's face.

We went to museums. I watched Nick take pictures of the art we were standing in front of. His images were one-dimensional. I looked at the canvas, noticing the layered swirls of paint.

It was only at night, lying in bed in some cheap hotel, that he looked me full in the face, his eyes unfocused, his body moving against mine. When he was done, he gave that same satisfied sigh he gave after texting.

We had a month left in our trip, before we looked for jobs, faced the future. Lake Como was our last stop. I'd seen pictures of the still lake, mountains in the background, buildings the color of parchment paper. Lake Como was beautiful, but it was the smells that intrigued me, the dank scent of the water, the sweet bougainvillea, the sharp espresso. I took it in, watching Nick's fingers dart back and forth as he played a video game.

Our waiter looked at me and Nick appraisingly. I looked back and shrugged. He brought me a plate of cookies I didn't order. I wrote my phone number on the napkin and slipped it into his breast pocket. Nick's phone trilled–high score.

Later, I watched as Nick walked dangerously close to the water's edge, texting. That evening, we sat in the town square. I watched the passeggiata, the evening walk. The waiter, now in jeans, approached and extended his hand. I took it. His hand was warm. We walked slowly away from where Nick sat on the bench, his face peering at his screen.

"Ba ba," I called to him over my shoulder. I didn't look back.

Kodachrome

Mama never knew about the pictures, the ones I found, the one I took, or the one that was taken of me. Her idea of a picture was the family photo in the Slocum Baptist Church directory, all of us with perfectly combed hair and wearing the same fake smile.

I found the magazine during spring-cleaning. It lay under my parents' mattress, pinned against the hard, metal box spring. There was a lady on the front in her nightie, and not one of those flannel ones I wear in the wintertime.

Despite being well worn, its pages were still glossy. When the light hit the page, it left a shine that reminded me of the sun hitting the window of Goodies Candy store in the late afternoon.

Inside, naked women were on their knees, lying on shag carpets, sprawled across modern furniture with their legs wide open. I saw the colors—bright red lipstick, raven black and golden blond hair—and every shade of pink.

I'd seen Mamma's body plenty of times—interrupting

her bath by perching on the toilet, lid down, to tell her about what had happened in school that day. Compared to these women, Mamma looked faded, used up, stretched out.

I'd take the magazine out when Mamma was at her card party or the grocery. I was always careful to put it back exactly in the same place.

We had just gotten a Kodak Instamatic with Magicube flash. I loved snapping the small glass cube with the sketch of the sun on it into place. I'd look through the viewfinder and expect to see something extraordinary. What I saw was Mamma and Daddy, same as ever, arms around each other, smiling at the camera. I'd wait until they started fidgeting, hoping to uncover something new. The pictures were nothing special, except sometimes their eyes were red.

Later, I would refer to my parents as traditional, but when I was twelve, they just seemed unbearably dull. My mamma had been a Home Ec major at University of Kentucky where she learned to make a perfect piecrust. Daddy loved walking in the woods and spent hours in the basement separating screws by size and placing them into empty coffee cans.

The thought of them doing what the pictures suggested was beyond imagining. If they had to do it, I was sure my mamma would imagine assembling a perfect casserole, and my daddy would be thinking of what lay beneath the hood of his car.

Slocum, where I'd lived forever, was especially boring. I was plain old Hannah Starnes with dirty blond hair and long legs that make me look like a stork. If only I could get a picture that showed my true colors.

***

One Sunday, I faked sick by holding a warm washcloth to my forehead for fifteen minutes. It's not bad, but she's warm, Mamma told Daddy. They decided I should stay home.

I snuck the instamatic upstairs and took a picture of myself. I lay back on the bed and pulled up my t-shirt. My sweat-covered hands shook. Point. Aim. The camera slipped from my fingers as I pressed the button. Pop. Our last flashcube gone. I used up the rest of the roll taking pictures of our cat Max lying in the sun on our front porch.

I rode my bike to Southpoint and paid my own money to get the pictures developed. My picture was a blur. I wanted to believe that the smudge of pink I saw was my nipple.

That was the year Jasper Macks came to town. He was different with his beard and the jacket with the elbow patches. Miss Allen, the school librarian, said he was famous for taking pictures of the war in Vietnam. He was traveling across the country taking pictures for the bicentennial.

He showed up at a church supper with his camera and spent almost the whole time walking from table to table introducing himself.

I watched him sitting on a park bench taking pictures of the garden club ladies working on the beds of petunias. On Saturday, Jasper Macks stood on the bleachers taking shots of the boys scattered across the dusty-brown baseball diamond.

He almost got a picture of Abby Linder as she decorated the window of the candy store. She held a large model of a lollipop in one hand and wagged her finger at Jasper with the other hand. He shrugged and moved slowly down the street in search of another subject.

He was even in the graveyard as my friends and I played hide and seek, our stealthy movements accompanied by the click of his camera.

I jumped from behind a gravestone and made a face for the camera—eyes crossed, tongue to the side. His laugh was rich and deep. I laughed too. He raised his camera and looked at me through the viewfinder. I stuck my tongue out and then hopped on my bike and headed home.

I saw him again on a bench outside of Goodies. He let me touch the camera, hold it to my eye. The town looked different through that lens—the courthouse, library, even the grocery store was important. Afterward, I gave him some Good and Plenty. He ate every one.

From then on, Jasper Macks and I were friends. He told me about lenses and apertures, and I introduced him to Bottle Caps and Jujubes.

He told me he was from *Bahston*. He said it just like that. I asked if that was near Boston, and he laughed his big laugh. I liked the look on his face when he saw something he wanted to capture and the way he waited for just the right shot. I'd watch him shifting from foot to foot until I heard the click.

Jasper Macks wanted to take my family's picture. I knew he

would be able to help me see my colors. I told him Mama said to come on Wednesday afternoon. That was the day she put on her fancy clothes and had lunch with friends in Andersonville.

***

Wednesday afternoon I put on a pair of Mama's high heels and wobbled over to the closet and picked out my prettiest dress, the one with a princess neckline dotted with small yellow flowers.

I felt grown up letting Jasper into the house.

Our living room had a bay window. Jasper said the light was good and set up his camera there. I looked around— polished wood floors, our old couch covered with a crocheted throw. No white rugs, shag carpeting, and leopard print. This would have to do.

"Where are your folks?" he asked.

"They probably got delayed at the hardware store. Why don't you get a shot of me to warm up?"

I stood in front of the window, swaying a bit on the high heels. When Jasper leaned down to take the lens off his camera, I slid my dress off. The air felt cold on my breasts. Jasper looked up, his eyes filled with surprise.

He told me to get dressed. I reached back and grabbed the throw from the couch, and wrapped it around my bare shoulders. The throw smelled of popcorn and cherry soda. Suddenly shy, I folded my arms in front of me. I felt the warmth of the sun as it shone through the window behind me, illuminating my colors.

I smiled at Jasper and heard the click of his camera. He took several shots.

Then it was over.

***

With her arms crossed, covered with the Afghan, Jasper could see the woman she would become. She looked him right in the eye, her chin up, a slight smile on her lips. The bright light shone in through the bay window, illuminating her. He took the picture quickly, praying that her parents wouldn't drive up.

"Why did you take your clothes off?' he asked.

"I want to be seen in all my colors," she said.

It was a curious answer, one he didn't understand.

The picture of her standing in the window would become his favorite from his time on the road, capturing her strength, innocence, and possibility.

"They aren't due anytime soon, are they?" Jasper asked.

"No," Hannah admitted.

Jasper packed up his camera as Hannah put her dress back on.

***

I expected to feel different, older, special, somehow, but I didn't. I wondered about the picture he took of me, if my colors had shone through.

School began again in late August. I stopped looking at the magazine. The instamatic gathered dust in the closet and was replaced by other passions—a new transistor radio and the music of Elton John. I almost forgot about Jasper all together.

***

When I was a senior, my class took a field trip to the Indianapolis Museum. As I walked through the museum, I saw Jasper's name over the door of a gallery. There was a special exhibit of his work.

I saw a picture of a toddler building a sand castle, Terri from the diner holding a plate of pancakes, and Pete Phillips standing in the forest with steam rising from his outstretched hands and a look of bliss on his face. Then I glanced at the hollowed out frame of a burning barn with flames still rising and a boy standing in the doorway covering his eyes.

My photograph was in the right corner. It was smaller than I thought it would be. I stood wrapped in the old blanket, the sun forming a halo behind me. It was a good likeness. I looked hopeful, expectant. But, I never did get to see my colors. The picture was in black and white.

Swimming

Huck Starnes was working the register at Slocum Hardware when he realized that everyone was dying before his eyes. His old coach Bill Barnes had just passed from pancreatic cancer, just a year after losing his wife to breast cancer. Abby Linder, who owned Goodies Candy Store and came in for pipe cleaner, was slightly bent at the shoulders, which gave one the impression that she was forever looking for a lemon drop that had rolled onto the floor. Even Miss Allen, the pretty librarian who loved wooden clothespins, had begun to develop a kind of squareness to her jaw that might move someone to call her a "handsome woman."

He felt it too. His knees ached after playing basketball. He wasn't regular anymore. It took him a lot longer to get worked up about Linda, his high school sweetheart and wife of 25 years. He still kept their weekly date, even if it meant he had to spend some time in the bathroom with his magazines beforehand.

What was it about those women in the photographs? Was

it that they seemed full of desire? Or maybe that they weren't around to ask him to mow the lawn or make sure the gutters didn't fall down?

If one of those women approached him on the street, he'd cringe at the thought of exposing his round belly to her—or worse—bending his head down to nuzzle her breasts and showing his ever-widening bald spot.

He loved the familiarity of his wife's body. He'd trace his fingers across the moles on her shoulder and knew just what to do with his tongue to get her breath to quicken. But he remembered a time, pre-Linda, when he was all curiosity and had never even touched a woman.

***

Annette Allen came to Slocum to nurse a broken heart. She had been in Louisville, going to library school when she met Jack Dant, a Pittsburgh boy who had been drafted and ended up at Fort Knox. Jack had dark hair cut close to his head and dark eyes. Jack had the full lips of a woman, but he talked like a sailor. Jack drank tea, not coffee, and read Ernest Hemingway.

When he was on furlough, Jack hung out at the Tip Top, a diner on Third Street with red leather booths and a small metal jukebox for each table. Annette would turn the wheel slowly, reading each song title as she ate her tuna on white bread with catsup.

Ella Fitzgerald was singing "All the Things You Are" when Jack passed Annette's table one afternoon.

"Jesus, what is that?" he asked, pointing to her sandwich.

"Good afternoon to you too," she said, turning back to the jukebox.

"Really, what is that?"

"Are you writing a book? It's a sandwich," she said slowly, looking at him with annoyance.

"What's in it?"

"If you must know, it's tuna salad on white with lettuce and catsup. My father created it. He calls it the 'summer swim.'"

He slid into the booth across from her. She made a show of looking at the jukebox.

"I'll have what she's having," he told the waitress.

***

Sam Sunderland had moved his family to Louisville and opened a successful retail store. They kept a "summer home" in Slocum; although, as time passed, they spent less and less time there. They finally decided to rent the place out to the new librarian at the high school.

The Sunderland house was just outside of town down a series of narrow gravel roads flanked by trees. Just when you were convinced there was nothing there, the road curved, and around the curve and down a quarter of a mile, the road ended at a little yellow cottage with light blue shutters.

The floor was made of thin planks of honey-colored hardwood, which reflected the light from the windows. The living room had built-in bookshelves, and the kitchen had a wooden bin built into the right corner. Someone had burned the words "potatoes" into the bin. There were lace curtains on the windows. The bedroom was dark and cool with a fan on the ceiling.

The bathroom was wood paneled and held a claw foot tub. Large, antique glass windows, wavy with age, looked out onto the woods. They were covered with sheer curtains that showed the pattern of the sun on the trees that edged the woods outside.

When she saw how beautiful the bathroom was, Annette Allen sat on the floor and wept.

***

Huck had been wandering in the woods after school—that was all. He'd walk the trails and try to figure out which animals had been there by their scat. He'd spent most of that afternoon doing nothing, following his thoughts like butterflies.

The sun was starting to set when he took the path that led to the old Sunderland place. Breaking through the woods, he was startled by what he saw. It was his own private movie theater, the window a screen. Behind the sheers, he could see the silhouette of a naked woman standing in a tub running a washcloth over her curves and valleys. He grew warm from the inside out. He stood behind a tree and watched until she covered herself with a towel. It was only later that it occurred to him that it was Miss Allen, the new librarian with the pretty face and sad smile.

***

Annette had known girls for whom losing their virginity was like winning a beauty pageant. They had been chosen, crowned. She was more interested in doing the choosing. She imagined her first time would be with a kind boy who would be as terrified as she was. They would take the leap together and muddle their way. It would create an unbreakable bond that would last them the rest of their lives.

Later, with three kids, the couple would be adept at pleasing each other, and they would laugh tenderly at their early fumblings. She never imagined that losing her virginity would be like buying a used race car, something shiny and sleek on the outside but broken deep inside.

***

Huck hadn't done it yet, though he and Linda had come close. It was the only thing his friends talked about—going all the way. They devised elaborate plans that ranged from charming a girl with candy to serving her a milkshake laced with oysters, which were supposed to be an aphrodisiac.

"Would you like to get into the back seat?" Linda asked when they were making out in his father's Ford Fairlane.

"No," said Hank. "I want to stay up here with you."

Linda doubled over in laughter. Hank blushed and looked away. Linda whispered, "Sorry."

Then she took his hand and guided it inside her panties. She let him keep it there for a full minute.

***

Jack Dant had her up against the wall in the hallway, arms

above her head as he ran his hands down her sides. She suppressed a giggle. Laughing would make Jack furious, and she knew not to make Jack furious. Annette had laughed at him one Saturday when he backed into a tree, and he got out of the car and bent a young sapling with his hands until he broke it across the middle.

They had been seeing each other for a month now, which constituted him walking her home from library school and putting his hands all over her the minute the door closed behind them. He looked like Tony Curtis but acted like Brando, rough and full of passion, a hurricane, a tidal wave. The waves were coming in, and she didn't know how to swim.

***

Linda's father died of a stroke on a Tuesday while mowing the lawn. He just waved at a neighbor, bent over to pick up a rock, and pitched over like a kid attempting a somersault. Linda stayed with her mother for as long as she could stand it. Her father's body was like the shell of a cicada—a hull, no life, no sound, his eyes empty and already starting to dry up.

She found Huck down by the creek and threw her arms around him. "Closer," she said, pressing herself into him, as if she could move through him and in doing so get something of her old self back. He held her close and stroked her. "Now," she said. They lay on a bed of dry leaves, the crackling sound the only evidence of their lovemaking.

***

When Annette opened the door to the apartment, Jack

was already inside, sitting in a chair in the dark, smoking. She felt unease in the center of her stomach. She wanted to turn and run, but she forced herself to enter the room. This was *her* apartment. Would Betty Davis run?

"It's time," Jack said.

"Pork chops or pot roast?" she asked, making her voice light.

Jack grabbed her arm and pushed her onto the bed. He pulled her skirt up and forced her legs apart with his own. "How do you like that, baby?" he asked.

She lay still, feeling the pressure and pain, her eye on a water stain shaped like a fish. She imagined it swimming away, across the ceiling and down the wall. Gone, gone, gone.

The next day, she moved into student housing with a roommate. She stayed away from the diner.

***

Huck had been surprised by fatherhood, the intensity of feeling it provoked, from the surge of protectiveness he felt when he held his daughter Hannah to the warm physicality of the weight of her body as she slept draped across his shoulder. It was as a father that he most fully felt like a man.

Then there were the magic days when, as a toddler, Hannah would sit on his lap and study him, running her small fingers over the tiny hairs on his nose, pulling at his earlobes, looking inside his ear as if the secrets of the world were there.

His own father had seemed like an alien invader who interrupted his peaceful days with his mother with demands for dinner and quiet. Sometimes he took Huck out into the backyard to toss the football, coaching him about the right way to hold the ball and when to let it go. Once, when his father patted his back, the gesture was so unexpected that Huck jumped like he'd been hit.

***

Sometimes Annette would play a game with herself when she looked out into the sea of students making their way down the hallway. She would look for one that looked like her, with blond hair, a slight upturned nose, her father's distinctive chin, just a shade of herself. She let herself imagine that the child she had given up would have ended up here, in this high school, in this small town.

Her child would stop and say, 'Hi, Mom' and act embarrassed when Annette smoothed down her hair. But no one stopped. The kids just walked on by, and she returned to the library, where she'd walk down the rows of books, placing each one in exactly the right spot so it could be discovered.

***

Huck liked the routine of work at the hardware store, every screw in the proper box, snow shovels out in the winter, rakes out in the fall. Hannah would stop in on her way home from school with her friends. They were like baby deer, awkward and beautiful. They would hit each other with fly swatters and pull out strips of paint colors in shades of purple and rose. Once he caught sight of Hannah in profile and saw Linda's young face in hers. It was scary, like occupying the future and the past at the same time.

***

She was retired now and spent her afternoons reading in a glider on the porch of her rented place by the woods. When Annette went into town, she noticed the faces of neighbors and former students, many grown and with kids of their own. They looked old. Even Huck Starnes. The open-faced boy who used to watch her bathing from the woods had a sunburst of wrinkles around his eyes now.

She went into the hardware store for a new soap dish. When Huck turned his attention to her, he spoke softly and kept his eyes down. When she told him what she was after, he brought a special soap dish out from the back of the store. It was delicate and shaped like a swan. She thought of the warm, soothing water of the bath and the sun-dappled curtains. He thought of the shape of her body and bird song. He wrapped the soap dish carefully in newspaper and placed it in a small white bag. It would hold the bar of white soap, newly unwrapped, that smelled of lilacs and morning dew.

Author's Note

The title story of this collection was inspired by the kidnapping of a local girl in my community when I was eighteen. I hope that story and the others help reflect the range of women's experiences and get close to touching the truth about the challenges and joys of being a woman, chief among them being seen, acknowledged, remembered, and heard.

I couldn't have completed these stories without the insight and careful attention of the women in my writing groups, Amanda Forsting, Mary Lou Northern, Kay Gill, Lynn Slaughter, Cameron Lawrence, Jenny Recktenwald, Mary Popham, Kelly Fordon and Linda Downing Miller.

I am also grateful to folks at Queens University-Charlotte, Fred Leebron, Michael Kobre, and Melissa Bashor, who developed a fantastic program with world-class teachers, and my mentors, David Payne, Nathaniel Rich, Steve Rinehart, and Susan Perabo for their insights and continued support. Thanks to Sheri Williams and Kim Coghlan for helping this book find its way into print.

Thanks to the Kentucky Arts Council for their support of my work, and Kentucky Foundation for Women and Elizabeth George Foundation, whose early grants provided vital encouragement.

Thanks always to Bud Morris for his unceasing support, encouragement, and good humor. Our time together is the great joy of my life. Special thanks to Amanda Forsting, our meetings feed my work and my soul.

I also want to thank my women friends, who bring such joy and kind attention to our time together. Thanks for seeing me. I see you.